Ten

Ten

LAUREN MYRACLE

DUTTON CHILDREN'S BOOKS
AN IMPRINT OF PENGUIN GROUP (USA) INC.

DUTTON CHILDREN'S BOOKS • A division of Penguin Young Readers Group

Published by the Penguin Group
Penguin Group (USA) Inc., 375 Hudson Street, New York, New York 10014, U.S.A.
Penguin Group (Canada), 90 Eglinton Avenue East, Suite 700, Toronto, Ontario M4P 2Y3,
Canada (a division of Pearson Penguin Canada Inc.) | Penguin Books Ltd, 80 Strand,
London WC2R 0RL, England | Penguin Ireland, 25 St Stephen's Green, Dublin 2, Ireland
(a division of Penguin Books Ltd) | Penguin Group (Australia), 250 Camberwell Road,
Camberwell, Victoria 3124, Australia (a division of Pearson Australia Group Pty Ltd) | Penguin
Books India Pvt Ltd, 11 Community Centre, Panchsheel Park, New Delhi - 110 017, India
Penguin Group (NZ), 67 Apollo Drive, Rosedale, Auckland 0632, New Zealand (a division
of Pearson New Zealand Ltd.) | Penguin Books (South Africa) (Pty) Ltd, 24 Sturdee Avenue,
Rosebank, Johannesburg 2196, South Africa
Penguin Books Ltd, Registered Offices: 80 Strand, London WC2R 0RL, England

This book is a work of fiction. Names, characters, places, and incidents are either the product
of the author's imagination or are used fictitiously, and any resemblance to actual persons,
living or dead, business establishments, events, or locales is entirely coincidental.

CIP Data is available.

Published in the United States by Dutton Children's Books,
a division of Penguin Young Readers Group
345 Hudson Street, New York, New York 10014
www.penguin.com/youngreaders

Designed by IRENE VANDERVOORT

Printed in USA   First Edition

ISBN 978-0-525-42356-0

10 9 8 7 6 5 4 3 2 1

DEDICATION

 To Frances Adams
and Chloe Chatfield:
Forever Full of Fabulosity!

ACKNOWLEDGMENTS

Big fuzzy thanks to all the usual crew, who will never be "usual" at all, thank goodness. My darlings, I love you.

Special thanks to: Barry "Care Bear" Goldblatt, the snuggliest, just-gotta-squeeze-him agent ever; Sarah Mlynowski, for her willingness to drop everything in order to read an early draft, and then—with her characteristic warmth and generosity— telling me not to worry, it was adorable, all was good; Lisa Yoskowitz, for educating me about Hanukkah and gelt; Liza Kaplan, for stepping in so smoothly and facilitating details large and small; Rosanne Lauer, for her fearless copyediting flair; Scottie Bowditch, for her passion and her proficiency, though more for her passion; Allison Verost, for loving Winnie and telling me so; and EVERYONE at Penguin/Dutton/ Julie's Private Boutique for being simply and plainly fabulous, especially—but not limited to—RasShahn Johnson-Baker, Irene Vandervoort, Steve Meltzer, Danielle Delaney, Eileen Kreit, Jennifer Bonnell, Linda McCarthy, and Casey McIntyre.

A ginormous dollop of icing-on-the-cake thanks to Ji Eun Kwak, for her *excellent* idea of sneaking Lars (as an adorable ten year old!) into the book; to ALL the sweetie-potato Winnie fans who emailed and wrote and said, "Please please please write another Winnie book!"; to the inimitable Beegee Tolpa, for bringing Winnie & Co. to life in beautiful color; and to Bob, for making me laugh, making me think, and making me shower and occasionally even take a day or two off. Well, an hour or two off. Well, for making me take at least twenty minutes to myself every so often, even when those twenty minutes seemed awfully hard to find.

And. Oh my goodness gravy. Above Winnie's house flies a fabulous pink biplane, skywriting the following in an endlessly repeating loop: Julie Strauss-Gabel, you are a goddess, an angel, an editor of astonishing brilliance. Thank you. Thank you. Thank you.

Ten

March

T HE THING ABOUT BIRTHDAYS is that they are shiny and sparkly and make the birthday girl feel special, no matter what. And guess what? Today *I* was the birthday girl! As of today, I was ten years old. As of today—oh my goodness gravy—I, Winnie Perry, was living in the Land of Double Digits.

It was a sparkly land, the Land of D-Squared. The air shimmered, making the faces of my sister and brother glow. The smell of breakfast filled my nostrils. Somewhere, unicorns frolicked. Maybe they were invisible, fine. But they frolicked anyway.

And even though today was a Wednesday, and my party wasn't until the weekend, I still felt special. Special*er*, even, because this way I'd get to have *two* days that were all about me—today *and* the day of my party! I didn't have to feel guilty, either, because Ty and Sandra would get special attention on their own birthdays. Everybody in the whole wide world had a birthday, so it was totally fair.

"Happy birthday, Winnie," Mom said, cruising to the

table and sliding a plate in front of me. On the plate was a microwaved sausage biscuit with a lit candle stuck in it.

"Awww!" I said.

"Wish! Wish!" Ty said. Ty was three-going-on-four and loved wishes. He loved everything, pretty much, except lice and occasionally dust balls, if the dust balls were small and dark and tumble-skittered across the floor in a might-be-a-spider sort of way.

"She can't wish on a sausage biscuit," Sandra told Ty. She turned to me, and her shiny hair did its Sandra-style swish. She had very pretty hair, my sister. "You can't wish on a sausage biscuit, Winnie."

I gave her a look. Just because she had pretty hair didn't mean she knew everything. Just because she was *thirteen* didn't mean she knew everything. Sometimes she did. *Lots* of times she did. But other times she just plain didn't.

"Actually, you are wrong about that," I said, and I screwed shut my eyes and made my wish: *Please, oh please, let this be my bestest birthday yet.*

I opened my eyes, pursed my lips, and blew a *whuh* of breath at that bitsy dancing flame. It went out, and a wisp of smoke curled upward from the wick.

"See?" I said.

"I see that you blew out a candle," Sandra stated.

"*On* my birthday, so that means a birthday wish. So plop on your head, you poopy girl."

Chocolate milk splurted from Ty's mouth. "Poopy," he repeated.

"Winnie, I hardly think that's how a ten year old should be talking," Mom said.

"Yeah, Winnie," Sandra taunted.

"Sandra, hush," Mom said.

"Yeah, Sandra. *Yeah*, poopy mouth."

"Poopy mouth!" Ty said.

"Both of you, hush," Mom said, gesturing at Ty to remind us of his little ears.

Ty raised his hand but didn't wait to be called on. "Whales poop, and so do gorillas," he said, only, *gorillas* came out as *guhwillas* because he hadn't mastered his *r*'s yet. "And so do spiders. I think." He pooched out his lips and twisted them to one side. "Do they?"

Mom *took a moment*, which she frequently did, and which involved pressing her fingers to her forehead and being very quiet in a way that suggested very loudly that we better be quiet, too.

She took a cleansing breath, signaling that she was done. "Winnie, you're growing up, which is great. But growing up does mean *acting* grown up."

Pleh, I thought, scrunching my nose.

"Being ten is a big deal. It means new responsibilities, new expectations—"

"New opportunities to be even weirder than you already

are," Sandra said, copycatting Mom's loving-but-earnest tone. She leaned across the table and took my hand. "New chances for people to mock you and call you Weirdy Pants."

"Sandra, don't call your sister Weirdy Pants," Mom said.

Ty giggled. "Weedy pants. Poopy pants. Plop on your pants, poopy head."

I fought not to let a grin sneak out. Sandra wasn't being mean. She was just trying to be funny. And she *was* funny. But if I laughed, she'd be *way* too pleased with herself, and her head would puff up like the marshmallows Ty liked to microwave. And those marshmallows were jumbo-sized to begin with.

Ty's marshmallows grew and grew and GREW as they spun around in the microwave. They grew until they were trembling white blobs, and then they exploded, splattering the walls of the microwave with sugary glue. Every so often one didn't explode, and on those occasions, the marshmallow said *pluh* in a sad marshmallow way and deflated. *Pluhhhhhhhhhhh*, until all that was left was a sad, flat marshmallow puddle.

I didn't want Sandra to explode *or* deflate. Usually. So I kicked her.

"Hey!" she exclaimed.

"Girls," Mom scolded.

"*I* think Sandra needs to remember that she's three years older than me and should be more mature," I said. "Don't you, Mother?"

"Indeed I do," Mom said.

I turned to Sandra and lifted my eyebrows. *So there*, my eyebrows said, because one of my many talents was my ability to hold entire conversations using nothing but the finely tuned squiggles of hair above my eyes.

Unfortunately, Sandra possessed the same gift. She lifted her eyebrows right back to say, *Oh, really? Like I care.*

Mom regarded me thoughtfully. "It might be worth addressing Sandra's point, however. Since the subject was brought up."

"I made a point?" Sandra said.

"No," I said. I had zero memory of any points Sandra might have made. "Sandra didn't make a point, did she, Ty?"

"I don't like spiders," Ty said. "They are nature, and nature stays outside."

"What point did Sandra make?" I asked Mom.

"Well, about . . ."

"About what?"

"About . . . well, about being . . ."

"Oh! I know!" Sandra exclaimed. "About people mocking you for being weird." She made a fist and drew it in to her side. "Score!"

"Hush your piehole," I told her crossly, because now my feelings *were* a little hurt. "Mom? You think people are going to mock me?"

"No, honey," Mom said. "No one is going to *mock* you."

"Other than me," said Sandra.

"But Winnie, it *is* true that you're . . ."

I waited for more words. More words didn't come, so I filled them in myself. "Adorable? Spunky? The genius of the family?"

"In a pig's eye," Sandra said under her breath.

I looked at Mom, and my stomach flip-flopped as I caught a glimpse of Concerned Mom, who was closely related to My-Baby's-Gotten-So-Big Mom, who was closely related to Oh-Sweetie-I-Wish-I-Could-Keep-You-Safe-in-a-Jar-Forever Mom.

She smoothed her features. "You're your own self, that's all. You're *unique*."

So much drama, for *that*?

"Well, of course, I'm unique," I said. "That's why my name is Winifred."

"Huh?" Sandra asked.

"Wi-ni-fred," I said again. "How many other Winifreds do you know, huh?" I didn't wait for a response. "None, that's how many, because Winifred is an extremely unique name."

Ty clinked his fork on his plastic plate. "Tyler James Perry," he announced, the *Perry* coming out as *Peh-wee*. "That's *my* cave name."

"Your cave name?" Mom said. "What's a cave name?"

"You mean your *whole* name," I told Ty. To Mom and Sandra, I said, "He doesn't mean his cave name. He means his whole name."

They regarded me blankly.

"Oh, come on," I said. "A hole, like a hole that you dig? And when it's in the ground, it's called a cave?"

"*Ah,*" Mom said. "Clever girl, my Winnie."

"That's me: clever, unique, *and* weird. And for the record? I like being me."

"Which is lucky, since you're stuck with yourself," Sandra said. She chomped off a bite of bagel. "Though *for the record*, Mom and Dad named you when you were just a baby, before you turned weird. And then later, you consciously decided to be weird, which is, itself, weird."

"Nope, I was born this way," I said.

She considered, then shook her head. "Nah. For a brief while you were normal. It was before you learned to talk." She shrugged. "But hey, I'm cool with your being weird. You might have to walk ten paces behind me at the mall, that's all."

"Oh, blah, blah, blah," I said.

"I think I've made things more complicated than they need to be," Mom said. She placed her hands on my shoulders. "All I wanted to say is that while being unique is wonderful, it can also be hard."

"But—"

"I'm not saying it *will* be, just that it *might* be. On the other hand, growing up itself is hard."

"Not for me, it's not. Growing up is awesome."

Mom chuckled. "Well, all right. And do you know what, Winnie? You are an amazing girl, and whatever comes your way, I know you can handle it."

"*Finally*, someone who's making sense around here!" I exclaimed. "And you're right, I can—and thank you for the lovely compliment. Thank you as well for my delicious breakfast, which you slaved over, and for my delicious chocolate milk, which you haven't poured yet, but which I know you will. Most of all, thank you for making me be born, and for naming me Winifred, and for letting me be unique."

I paused, knowing there was something I was forgetting, but unable to put my finger on it. Then it came to me. "*Oh.* And I know Dad helped out, so tell him thanks, too."

"Yes, ma'am," Mom said. She leaned over and kissed my cheek. "And Winnie? You are very welcome."

On Saturday, everyone pitched in to make our house look haunted, because that was the theme of my party. It was a haunted house party, with spiderwebs clinging to the ceiling and a fake black rat out front and scary *ooooo* sounds coming from a scary sounds CD Mom and Dad gave me, along with my own CD player. I'd asked for an iPod, but Mom and Dad were like, "Uhhhhh, *no*," so a CD player it was. Okay by me!

The scary sounds CD was excellent, but the best part of the haunted house was in our basement. It involved dry ice, extreme spookiness, and Sandra in an awesome black velvet witch dress with an even awesomer pointy black velvet hat.

The whole caboodle was going to scare everybody's pants off. I couldn't wait.

Amanda arrived first, because she was my best friend, and that's the way it was supposed to be. And the reason she was my best friend was because she liked my ideas and laughed at my jokes and was willing to Rollerblade when the Rollerblading mood struck us, even though we were both pretty bad and fell a lot.

She was also my best friend because she was purely and truly *nice*, from her skin all the way through to her bones. If she was a color, she would be daffodil yellow. If she was a flower, well, she'd be a daffodil. If she was anyone other than Amanda, then I would miss the real Amanda terribly without even knowing it. I wouldn't laugh nearly as much, or be nearly as silly, and I wouldn't have an adopted cat named Sweet Pea, who wasn't mine and didn't live at my house, but whom I got to share. It would be dreadful.

Chantelle showed up next. While Amanda and I had been friends since forever, Chantelle had come onto the scene in third grade, and she'd quickly become our second-best friend. She loved things like clothes and purses and makeup, even though she wasn't allowed to wear any yet except in her own house, just for fun. For me, clothes and makeup had nothing to do with fun, and purses were downright anti-fun. Blech! Even the word *purse* made me grimace.

But Chantelle was more than a purse-lover. She was funny and feisty, and when she disapproved of something, she cocked her hip and said, "Oh, nuh-*uh*." She also said, "How *rude*," if someone was being rude, and she huffed out the rude part with extreme huffiness. It made me giggle, even if I was the one who was supposedly being rude.

Maxine arrived soon after Chantelle, followed by Louise and Karen. Karen was supposedly Louise's best friend, but she was more like Louise's pet, kind of. Even though she was a real live girl like the rest of us.

The last girl to be dropped off was Dinah Devine. Dinah was round and oatmealy and never got a tan, even in the summer. I didn't say that to be mean. Unless, *yikes*. Was it mean? I didn't dislike Dinah. She was just nervous a lot of the time. Sometimes I worried that she might . . . break. Or cry. Or smile really big with her mouth, but not her eyes.

But I had to invite her to my parties whether I wanted to or not, because Mom made me. Dad and Mr. Devine worked together, that's why.

Everyone deposited their presents in the TV room, and while they were there, they stopped by the tattoo station, which Dad was in charge of. He used a wet paper towel to apply either a tiny skull, a spider, or a black cat on each girl's cheek—or, in Louise's case, all three. That was Louise in a nutshell. She was the sort of girl who wanted it all.

Then again, I made Dad put all three designs on me as well. I got him to do me early, since I was the birthday girl, and actually I sort of ended up with multiple tattoos of each, including ten spiders (because I was ten!) marching up my arm in a line.

Like I said, I was the birthday girl.

After tattoos, I led everyone to the top of the basement staircase. I glanced around and hollered, "Amanda, your presence is required!"

I wanted her up front with me. It was another best-friend thing.

"Burst my eardrum next time," Louise complained.

"Okay," I said.

Amanda weaved her way to me, and I took her hand. Even without additional party spookiness, the basement was already plenty spooky because of how old and unmodern our house was. The stairs were creaky and clompish, and sometimes there were dead roaches on them. Built into the wall along the side of the staircase was a hidden trapdoor, and if you opened it, all you saw was *dirt*. It was like peeking into a coffin . . . or peeking *out* of a coffin. *Shudder*.

"Is everyone ready?" I said. "If you're not, this is the time to speak up, especially if you have high blood pressure, extreme scaredy-cat-ness, or a tendency to faint. And if you're pregnant, or think you *may* be pregnant, you'll need to consult with your doctor before proceeding."

"Winnie," Amanda said, hip-bumping me.

"What?" I said. That's what the signs said at the rides at Six Flags. If only I owned a wooden cutout of a person holding up his hand to measure how tall kids were—that would have been hilarious! I could have placed it at the top of the staircase and made everyone get checked!

Oh, well. Next time.

Louise raised her hand.

"Yes, Louise?" I said.

"First of all, no, I'm not pregnant."

"Thank you, Louise," I said. "Thank you for clearing that up, even though I never actually thought you were."

"But I don't understand this whole haunted-house thing. Haunted houses are for Halloween."

Then why did you ask for three tattoos? I was tempted to ask, and I would have if I, myself, weren't also tattooed to the hilt.

"Haunted houses *are* for Halloween," I said. "You're right."

"Then why—"

"However!" I cried, whipping one finger high into the air. "They're not *just* for Halloween, now are they?" I took that finger and pointed it dead at Louise. "Do you think ghosts just lollygag about for the three-hundred-and-sixty-four days of the year that aren't Halloween?"

"Well—"

Jab went my finger. "Are witches not allowed out except on October thirty-first? Isn't that a little unfair?"

"I just—"

"Ex*act*ly," I said. My finger was a sword, and I the swordsman. *Swordsgirl*. Whatever. "So let's just keep our Negative Nelly thoughts to ourselves, shall we?" I waggled my eyebrows. "Unless you're *too afraid*? Is *that* what you're trying to say, Louise?"

She gave me a look, because we both knew she wasn't. Louise wasn't as brave as I was, perhaps, but she was certainly no chicken. Once she faked being sick during PE because she didn't want to play dodgeball. She said, "Oh dear, I feel faint," and she collapsed on the floor and didn't open her eyes even when people poked her. One girl even nudged Louise's ribs with her sneaker, and Louise still kept her eyes shut. And the girl with the sneaker was me.

I went back and forth between admiring Louise and finding her annoying. Often it was both.

"You are *so* weird, Winnie," she pronounced from her spot at the top of the staircase.

Karen giggled, *and so did Chantelle*. My stomach muscles fluttered, because was this what Mom meant about how life might be hard for a girl like me? A girl who was her own self, that is, and thought haunted houses in March were fine?

I glanced past my friends, anxiously seeking out Mom.

She was at the back of the group with Ty, and when our eyes met, she gave me a private, knowing smile. *We prefer the term *unique*, don't we?* her smile said. *Stand tall, my Winnie. You are fabulous, and I love you.*

My chest swelled. I stood tall. Shifting my gaze back to Louise, I said, "Of course I'm weird. You're just now figuring that out?" I clapped twice. "Now, enough with the chit-chat. This is serious business here, people."

I started down the basement stairs. We passed the secret trapdoor, and Amanda said, "Inside that door, there's dirt."

"Yep," I confirmed.

A few feet farther, the stairwell curved to the left, and the inside edges of the stairs grew narrower than ever.

"If you need to, you can hold onto the wall for balance," I said, demonstrating. The deeper we went, the cooler it got. The air smelled different, too.

At last I reached the bottommost stair. In front of me was the thick wooden door that led into the basement—or, as Mom and Dad called it, *the furnace room*. Because it wasn't a basement like normal people's basements. There were no Ping-Pong tables or flat-screen TVs or smooshy sofas. There was just . . . *dum dum dum* . . . the furnace: huge, ancient, and growly. And today, behind the furnace?

Sandra, lying in wait in her full witchy glory.

My heart pounded, and I already knew what was coming.

I waited until everyone was clumped together. I put my hand on the brass doorknob. "Ready?"

"You already asked us that, and *yes*," Louise said.

"I'm not," Dinah said, squeezing up next to me and Amanda. Her skin was moist, and she had a big grin on her face. Her chest went up and down, up and down. "It's not going to be bad, is it?"

"Well, yes, I'm afraid it is."

"No," Mom called from the back of the crowd. She held Ty in her arms since the stairs were so trippable. "Don't worry, Dinah. It's just for fun."

"*If* you consider terrible, scary things to be fun, she means."

"Ha ha," Dinah said. She honestly said those two words—*ha ha*, like that—and she tried to worm her hand in with mine and Amanda's. I shook her off, because three people can't hold hands. It doesn't work that way.

"You'll be fine, Dinah," Mom called.

"Here goes nothing," I announced. I twisted the knob, and we stepped as a many-footed creature into the nearly pitch-black room. The walls and floor were made out of concrete, like an underground cell. The only light came from the hallway behind us. In the far back corner, the furnace hissed.

"What's that?" Dinah squeaked.

"Oh . . . *nothing*," I said, implying that it was far from nothing and might even eat her.

I released Amanda's hand and faced the group. I stared at them vacantly.

"Come, leetle children," I said in a floaty, spine-tingling voice. I stepped backward, beckoning with twiglike fingers. "Come and *sssssee* what fate awaits you . . . *if* you dare."

"Mom?" Ty whispered loudly.

"Shhh," Mom said to Ty. To me, she said, "Winnie, take it down a notch."

She and Ty remained in the doorway as the rest of us moved deeper into the gloom.

Karen bumped into someone and yelped, and I laughed creepily. "*Yesssss. Yessssssss*, my darlings, you are right to be afraid."

"She's teasing," Mom told Ty. "She's still plain old Winnie. Right, Winnie?"

I was Winnie, yes. But "plain old"? Never. My spine tingled, and I laughed again.

Dinah hiccupped.

Louise said, "Karen, *ow*. Let go."

"What, I wonder, might be behind such a terrible thing as that?" I asked, indicating the furnace. "Eees it . . . a ghostling? A zombie? A donkey?"

"A *donkey*?!" Louise said.

Chantelle giggled, and I scowled, irritated at myself. I hadn't meant to say "donkey." I didn't know where that donkey came from.

I shook it off. Re-widening my eyes, I said, "Or . . . could it be . . . just *possibly* . . ."

"*Rwaarggghh!*" Sandra roared, flying out from behind the furnace. She did a banshee dance, squatting and hopping from one foot to the other. In one hand she held a fake iron kettle, which she swooped through the air. Misty, gray smoke curled up because of the dry ice inside it.

"*Rwaargh! Rwaargh!*" she cried, lunging toward us.

Dinah screamed. Karen screamed. We *all* screamed, and something winged through me that turned my giggle-scream into a real scream. The sound of it—coming from *me*, from my open mouth—made me scream even louder.

Ty started wailing, and Mom said, "Oh, Ty." I looked over to see Mom holding his body away from her. Her nice pants had a big dark spot on them, and Ty's jeans were dark, too.

He tried to muscle his way back against her upper body, burying his head between her head and shoulder.

"It's okay, buddy," Mom said. "But I think we should head back up, huh?" To me, she said, "Winnie? Maybe you should wrap it up, too."

"But *Mo-o-o-m*," I complained.

Dinah hiccupped. She hiccupped *again*, and Sandra dropped her witchy posture.

"Want me to scare you?" she volunteered matter-of-factly.

Amanda giggled, and just as Karen's initial scream had

made everyone else scream, Amanda's giggle triggered a domino spill of giggle-giggle-snort-laughs. Even for Dinah, and even for me. Especially for me.

Later, after everyone had gone home, I flopped onto my bed and gazed at the ceiling. I was feeling a bit blue because of my birthday being almost over. Also, I was feeling kind of . . . troubled. Had it been a good party or a bad party? Were haunted houses in March weird after all?

Well, yes, haunted houses in March *were* weird. But were they *too* weird? Was there such a thing as too weird after all?

At cake time, Louise pushed her slice away, claiming she only ate normal cake and not weird ghost-flavored cake. She also said black icing stunted kids' growth.

"So eat a piece from the middle," I told her, since only the ghostie's eyes and mouth were black. The rest was white. Anyway, the *shape* of the cake was a ghost, but the *flavor* was chocolate. And it was rude of Louise to say that with Mom right there, since Mom had baked and decorated the cake herself.

"No, thanks," Louise said, as in *the whole cake is weird and anyone who eats it will turn short and deformed, the end.*

Lying on my bed, I sent Louise a telepathic scowl. Then I got up and went in search of Sandra. Sandra would know if my party had been too weird or not, and I could trust her to tell me the truth. She wasn't the type of person who lied to make people feel better.

"Was my party weird or good?" I asked when I found her in the bathroom. She was brushing her teeth. Her mouth was frothy.

She shrugged. "Both."

"*Both?* How could it be both?"

She spat. "Winnie, think about it. With you, how could it *not?*"

"*Sandra.*"

"What?" She cupped up some water and rinsed her mouth. "You are a weird child. You will always be a weird child. Deal with it."

I put my hands on my hips. "Listen, you. I am *not* a child. I am *ten* now, and being ten means I am fully and completely a tween. Before you know it, I will even be . . . doing puberty and taking shaving lessons."

She met my eyes in the mirror. "You totally just proved my point, you know."

"Nuh-uh!" I cried. "You just don't want to admit that I'm growing up, but I am." She looked amused, so I stomped my foot. "I *am,* you big old . . . *you.*"

She turned from the sink and dried her hands on a towel. "Okay, okay," she said, giving in way too easily. "It's just . . . don't feel like you have to rush it, all right?"

"Meaning what?" I asked suspiciously.

"Meaning that you should take time to smell the roses. Or in your case, that disgusting perfume you made out of daffodils and grape juice."

"'Daffodil Delight,'" I said. I invented it in honor of Amanda, and it was *not* disgusting . . . although it was also not entirely *un*disgusting. "And I'm still perfecting the formula."

"Okeydoke," she said. She patted my head.

I ducked away from her. "Stop agreeing with me!"

"Winnie, chill. All I'm saying is that growing up is fine, and it happens whether you want it to or not, but it isn't all it's cracked up to be."

"It is for me," I argued.

"Lucky you. Remember that when something hard comes along, 'kay? And remember that I tried to warn you."

"I will, and it won't, and you did not!" I insisted. Then I got confused in my head. *"Aaargh!"* I cried, spinning on my heel and marching out of there.

Back in my room, I went to my desk and got out a piece of strawberry-bordered notepaper out of the strawberry stationery set Chantelle had given me. It included a strawberry-scented pen, a strawberry pencil, and an adorable eraser that looked just like a strawberry, only smaller.

"Growing up is all it's cracked up to be," I wrote. "And being weird is much more fun than not being weird, and so is being unique, and if anything hard ever does come along, then who cares? I'll handle it, just like Mom said. I can handle anything, and the reason why is because I am me and I am ten and I am awesome. And maybe that sounds braggy, but I don't mean it that way. I'm simply telling the truth, the whole truth, and nothing but the truth."

I tapped the end of the pen against my chin. Then I leaned back over the paper. "P.S. Black icing does NOT stunt your growth."

Full of righteous determination, I stood up, grabbed my chair, and dragged it over to my bed. I lifted it on top of my bed and positioned it near the headboard. Holding my note in my teeth, I climbed onto the chair, which rocked like a boat in heavy seas. S-l-o-w-l-y, I straightened up.

Whoa! Wobble! I crouched to regain my balance, then tried again. I stood on my tiptoes, and felt way high up along the molding that joined my wall to my ceiling.

Yes, I thought when my fingers found what I was searching for. It was a hollow space in the crown molding, and I'd discovered it purely by luck one day. I'd been throwing mini-marshmallows into the air and catching them in my mouth, or trying to. Only one marshmallow flew up and disappeared . . . and *that's* how I found my secret hiding spot.

I took the note out of my mouth and dropped it inside the hole. If I ever needed a reminder that growing up was something to be glad about, well, now I'd know where to go.

My eyebrows went up, because I had an idea for how to make it even better. Louise had given me a Hershey's bar as part of my present, and I eased off the chair, hopped off my bed, and grabbed it. Then I repeated the whole wobbly process, dropping the candy bar into the hollow space along with the letter.

Now if I ran into a time of trouble, I'd have my note *and* a chocolate bar to cheer me on. Hurrah! As a bonus, it would be a chocolate bar that came from Louise, which would prove my point even more. I wasn't sure how, just that it would.

I heard footsteps on the stairs, so I scrambled off my bed and lugged my chair back over to my desk. I scurried into bed right as Mom and Dad came in to say good-night. I pretended I'd been lying there peacefully for ages. I was a peaceful little angel.

"Did you have a good day, Winnie-cakes?" Dad said.

"Alas, I did not," I said, as I was still in a mood of feeling bound to tell the truth. Also because it was fun to mess with Mom and Dad.

Mom stepped closer, concerned. "Oh, sweetie. You didn't have a good birthday?"

"Nope," I said. I waited one second, two seconds . . . and then I couldn't stand it anymore. "I didn't have a good birthday. I had a *great* birthday. Wanna know why?"

"By all means," Dad said.

"Because this is going to be a wonderful year, and I'm not even kidding." I broke into a big, angelic grin. "Being ten *rocks*."

April

O NCE UPON A TIME there was a little mousie, and it was just a baby, and Amanda's BAD DADDY killed that little mousie just because he lived in the Wilsons' basement. Or she. She might have been a girl mousie. We didn't know. But that was very very bad of Mr. Wilson, Amanda and I thought, because how did the mousie know it wasn't allowed to live in their basement?

After Mr. Wilson killed the mousie, he chucked it into the backyard and just . . . left it there! Which was heartless and terrible and cruel, and we told him so.

"Well, girls, I'm sorry I upset you," he said, washing his hands at the kitchen sink. "But we can't have our house overrun with mice. Amanda, do you want mice setting up quarters in your bedroom?"

Amanda's mouth, which was open in a getting-ready-to-scold position, closed shut.

I elbowed her.

"Leaving mouse droppings in the carpet?" Mr. Wilson said. "Having mouse babies in your pillows?"

I elbowed her harder. "A*manda*," I whispered-yelled.

"Mouse droppings?!" she whispered back. "That would be freaky!"

"I wish I didn't have to kill the little fellow, either," Mr. Wilson said. "You can move the body to the trash can if you prefer. Just be sure to use a paper towel."

Amanda and I looked at each other.

"Or don't," he said. "My guess is that Sweet Pea will be happy to take care of it."

"Dad, *no*, and that's not funny," Amanda told him. I agreed. If I had a beautiful cat like Sweet Pea, I wouldn't want her to eat a dead mouse and have dead-mouse breath, either. Also I wouldn't want to be licked by Sweet Pea for a *long* time afterward.

"I didn't say it to be funny." He turned off the faucet. "It's the circle of life, that's all."

"Come on, Amanda," I said, dragging her out of the kitchen. We marched across the yard, scanning the grass until we found the little mousie's body. It looked kind of . . . yucky, and not all that cute, to tell the truth. The *If You Give a Mouse a Cookie* mouse was a lot cuter. I felt bad for thinking that, though.

"We need to name him," I said. "How about Henry?"

"Okay," Amanda said.

"Poor Henry," I said.

"What if Henry was his mother mouse's only living

child, and now he's dead, and her mouse husband is dead, too, and now she's a poor childless widow?" I said.

"Poor Henry's mom!" Amanda said.

"We have to bury him. It's our duty."

Amanda nodded. "I'll go get you a shovel. Or a spoon, a big-sized spoon."

She dashed off, and I thought it was a little funny— not ha ha funny, but more growly hmmmph funny—that Amanda automatically assumed that I'd be the one to dig Henry's grave.

But I did. I dug a hole with the spoon Amanda brought me, and then I used the spoon again to nudge Henry in. Henry's body moved—of course it did, because I moved it—but it was freaky-creepy-gross, and we both squealed and jumped away. Then I had to go back and push all the dirt back on top of him, which made me squeal and do the shudder dance again.

"You are so brave," Amanda said when we were inside washing up.

"I know," I said, panting.

"No, really," she insisted, as if we'd both barely escaped with our lives.

"I know. Really."

"Girls, that was very nice of you to bury that mouse," Amanda's mom said, clicking into the kitchen in high heels. "And Amanda, I told your father that he should have taken care of it himself."

"I did take care of it!" Mr. Wilson called from their den. "Do you want mice having babies in your pillow, Theresa?"

Theresa—otherwise known as Mrs. Wilson, or Mrs. Amanda's Mother—ignored him. "I would like to take you two out for a ladies' lunch to thank you. How does that sound?"

"Yay!" I said.

"Yes!" Amanda said.

"You've both washed your hands?" Mrs. Wilson said. "On the backs, on the sides, under your fingernails?"

We nodded.

She grabbed her purse from the counter, along with her jingly key chain with the jeweled butterfly dangling from it. "Then let's go."

We went to the mall, and we had the *best* time. We had chicken salad at a fancy restaurant called the Tea Room, and actually I didn't like the taste of it, because I don't like chicken salad. Or any kind of salad. Or anything involving mayonnaise.

I did like sitting with Amanda and her mother and using nice posture, however. And we had mango sorbet for dessert, and it was just plain delicious.

Then we went "window shopping," as Amanda's mom called it, and all the shop ladies smiled at us and told Mrs. Wilson what adorable daughters she had.

"Are you twins?" the lady at Tiffany's said. Tiffany's

was an extremely fancy jewelry store. It scared me to walk in there, it was so fancy.

"No," Amanda said, while at the same time, I said, "Yes."

We looked at each other and giggled.

"This one's mine," Mrs. Wilson said, claiming Amanda with a hug. Then, with her other arm, she hugged me. "This one's a loaner. But I love them both."

My heart sang. I was Amanda's twin, almost!

I felt so happy and proud that when we went to the next store, I did something embarrassing. We were smelling perfumes when a salesclerk approached us with a smile. My eyes happened to latch onto hers before anyone else's did, so she aimed her words at me.

"Hello there," she said. "And how are you today?"

"Oh, I'm beautiful," I replied sunnily.

"Winnie!" Amanda said. She looked at me with a shocked face, and I realized what I'd done. Instead of answering the saleslady's question, I'd basically said, *Hello there, pleasant saleslady. I sure am beautiful, aren't I?*

I made a shocked face back at Amanda, with an added layer of horror since I was the one who said it.

"I mean . . . I mean . . ."

Amanda started giggling, and it turned into a full-out giggle fit, and soon her giggling set *me* off. My giggling got so bad that I could hardly breathe, only I *had* to breathe, because I was a human and not a sea creature.

I inhaled a great sucking breath, and Amanda slumped helplessly against the perfume counter.

"You sound like a dying walrus!" she managed.

"I do not!" My stomach muscles hurt from laughing so much. "Anyway, how do *you* know what a dying walrus sounds like?"

I tried to wind down, but as I did, I exhaled really loudly—which, of course, made me sound like a dying walrus again. Which made me think of poor dead Henry, which made me clutch Amanda and say, "Poor dead Henry!", which made the whole cycle start all over again.

For the rest of the day, all either one of us had to do was mention the name Henry, or say pitifully, "Poor little fella," and off we'd go, back into Crazy Giggle Land.

It was the most fun I'd ever had at the mall, especially since Mrs. Wilson didn't get fed up with us or anything. Instead, she took us to Amanda's favorite store and let us both pick out "a little something."

"To buy?" I said.

"No, to steal," Amanda said.

I felt a blush coming on, so to cover for it, I made puppy-dog eyes and said, "Poor, poor Henry. Then he'd have to go to the jailhouse."

It made no sense, but *say la vee,* as people on TV shows sometimes said. Which also made no sense. *Say la vee?* Why would anyone say "la vee"? What was a "la vee," even?

At the end of the day, Mom came to get me. I said good-bye to Amanda, and I told Mrs. Wilson thanks for having me, just like Mom had taught me.

"Anytime," Mrs. Wilson said. To Mom, she added, "Your daughter is a delight. I just love the friendship our girls have, don't you?"

I floated all the way out of the Wilsons' front door, loving life. I loved Amanda, and I loved my new bracelet with a peace sign on it, and I loved Mrs. Wilson for buying it for me. More than that, I loved Mrs. Wilson for just being so *nice*.

Waiting in the car was a grumpy Sandra. "What took you so long?" she complained.

I ignored her. Ty was across from me in the backseat, asleep in his car seat, and I grabbed his warm little hand and held it. His fingers were sticky, but holding his hand helped keep my glowy feeling going.

"I love Amanda's mom," I said as Mom turned on the car.

"Awesome. Thanks for sharing," Sandra said.

"She's so nice," I went on. "She's the nicest mom I know, and she never uses a sharp voice." I sighed. "I wish she was my mom."

Sandra craned her neck and looked at me. She looked at me *hard*, as if to say, *Really? Really, Winnie?*

At first I didn't get it. Then I did, and my heart skipped a beat.

"So you'd give Mom up for Mrs. Wilson?" Sandra said, just to drive the point home. "Nice. Bet that makes Mom feel really good."

"Wait, I just said that *accidentally*." I gulped. "Mom?"

"I know," Mom said. She paused. "But sweetie, you do know that Amanda is an only child."

I drew my eyebrows together. What did that have to do with anything?

"I like Theresa, too," Mom continued. "You know what, though? I bet even she uses a sharp voice every so often. Just not when you're there, perhaps."

I tried to imagine Mrs. Wilson speaking sharply. I couldn't.

"Anyway, you're part of *this* family," Mom said. She glanced at me in the rearview mirror, and my heart hurt. She smiled, but her eyes had a smidgen of sad-Mommy in them. "What would I do without my Winnie?"

That night I told Mom again that I really and truly didn't mean what I'd said. I couldn't stand the thought that I'd hurt her feelings. I would never want to hurt her feelings!

She kissed my forehead and said, "I love you, Winnie, and I know you love me. Don't worry, baby."

But I did.

The next day was a Sunday, and I made her a bookmark that said, "To the Best Mom Ever." On it I drew a picture of her reading a book, because she loved reading just like I did, and I laminated it using lots and lots of Scotch tape.

"It's beautiful," she said. "I'll keep it forever."

On Monday, as Sandra, Ty, and I were eating breakfast, I complimented Mom's blouse.

"Thank you, Winnie," she said from the sink, where she was rinsing dishes. She rarely sat down and ate with us kids on school mornings. Dad left for work before we even woke up, which meant Mom was on her own to get us up and dressed and fed *and* have time to run upstairs and "throw a little makeup on," as she put it.

"You really are the best mom in the universe," I said. "And the prettiest. And the nicest."

"Laying it on pretty thick," Sandra remarked. "Are you feeling guilty about something? Is that why?"

I glared at her. *"No."*

"Are you sure?"

"You just hush." I took a big bite of sausage biscuit as if somehow that would silence her, but all it did was keep *me* from being able to say anything when she kept right on talking.

"It's just that you said something totally different two days ago," she said. "It was after we picked you up from Amanda's. We were driving home, and you said . . ." She tapped her lower lip. *"Hmm.* What was it you said?"

"Sandra," Mom said in a warning tone.

Yeah, I tried to say, but my mouth was too full. I chewed

and chewed, while at the same time giving Sandra an eyeball thrust to say, *Shush, AND I MEAN IT.*

Finally I was able to swallow. I washed everything down with a long swig of orange juice, which I sucked up using a shorter-than-normal plastic straw. A full-length straw would have been too tall for my glass, so Mom had snipped an inch off the bottom to make it fit.

Mom did that because she knew how much I loved straws. She kept a whole container of them on the kitchen counter, and she made sure we never ran out. She always remembered to plunk one into my glass, and if the glass was on the small side, she always cut the straw down to size.

She did *all that* for me.

Suddenly it was hard to make my throat work, even with my orange juice right there.

I needed to think about something else. I plucked my straw from my glass and held it between two fingers, pretending it was a cigarette. I inhaled, then exhaled with a loud puff. I did this several more times.

"You're going to turn your lungs black, you know," Sandra commented.

"Smoking is disgusting," I said. "Don't you think, Mom? I'm *so* glad you're not a smoker."

Mom smiled as she put a plate in the dishwasher. "I agree, and I'm glad you're not a smoker, either. I hope you never will be."

"I won't," I promised.

"Does Amanda's mom smoke?" Sandra asked.

I wanted to kick her. Instead, I turned very deliberately to Ty and said, "Ty, my darlingest brother, would you like a bite of yummy sausage?"

"Trying to change the subject," Sandra sang under her breath.

I pinched off a piece of sausage and held it out. Ty frowned.

"Do I like yummy sausage?"

"Yes, Ty, you love yummy sausage, just like you love me, because I'm your favorite sister."

Sandra snorted, and I wished she would turn into smoke and disappear. Then I truly would be Ty's favorite sister, because he'd only have one to choose from. He'd have one sister—me—and I would have zero sisters. And guess what? I would be *fine* with that.

It hit me that if Mom wasn't my mom, Sandra really *wouldn't* be my sister, and Ty wouldn't be my brother. My ribs tightened, because the possibility of no Ty wasn't allowed in my world.

As for Sandra . . .

Usually I felt lucky to have her for a sister, because she was so much fun. Like when she pretended to be a witch for my birthday party, or when we did bottom-bouncing from the top of the stairs to the bottom, and she went "*ow ow ow*" to the exact beat of the bouncing.

But sometimes? When Sandra did things on purpose to upset me? I almost hated her.

Ty leaned toward me and touched the piece of sausage with his tongue. *"Yuck,"* he said, batting it out of my hand and onto the floor. "I do *not* love yummy sausage."

"See?" Sandra said. "Ty doesn't love yummy sausage, just like you don't love—"

"I said hush!" I cried. Tears stung my eyes, and I *did* hate her. I really and truly hated her, and if that made me a horrible person, too bad.

"Girls," Mom said, leaving the dishes and striding to the table. "Sandra? Drop it."

"But—"

"Drop it," Mom repeated.

I blinked and dug my fingernails into my palms. I would dig my fingernails into Sandra if I could.

Mom placed her hands on my shoulders. "Winnie, would you come with me to the den, please?"

"Why?" I said.

"Just for a chat."

My heart hammered. I kept my gaze on my plate.

She squeezed my shoulder. "Come on, baby. Everything's going to be okay."

I got up, and Mom and I walked together across the kitchen. At the doorway, I spun on my heel.

"No listening," I warned.

"Like I'd want to," Sandra said.

"Eat your breakfast, Sandra," Mom snapped.

Sandra flinched. I was glad.

"You too, Ty," Mom said. "We need to leave for school in ten minutes."

In the den, Mom took a seat on the sofa and patted the cushion beside her. I sat next to her. At first I stayed rigid, like a statue, but when she touched me, I melted and let her pull me close. She stroked my hair. I took a shuddery breath.

"What's up, buttercup?" she said gently.

I let my gaze go blurry, so that what I saw was Mom plus sofa plus a strand of my own brown hair, only all jumbled together. It was like one of those paintings made up of dots and lines and squiggles, so that when you looked at it, you didn't see a farmhouse or an apple or whatever. All you saw was a smeary mess.

"Sandra is mean," I said. "She was trying to make me say something when she knew I didn't want to. And the thing I didn't want to say . . ."

I didn't finish. I shut my eyes and pressed against her.

"Sandra's not mean," Mom said, because she had to. "But she *did* take things too far."

"Will you give her a talking-to?"

"Yes, I'll give her a talking-to." She paused. "What about you and me? Do *we* need to have a talk?"

I didn't answer.

"Not a bad talk," Mom clarified. "Just a clear-the-air talk. What do you say?"

I said nothing, that's what. We sat on the couch, and Mom played with my hair, and for several seconds she let me be. Then she gave me a squeeze and nudged me back into a sitting position.

"Will you look at me?" she said.

I didn't want to, but I made myself.

"Winnie, I love you," she said, stroking my cheek with the back of her hand. "You are my ten-year-old girl, and you are growing up beautifully, and I am *so* glad you're my daughter."

"And I'm so glad you're my mom," I told her, my chest swelling up like a balloon. I flung myself on her. "You're the best, most perfect mom in the whole world, and I'm *not* just saying that."

She smiled. "How about this: I'm the perfect mom for *you*, and Theresa is the perfect mom for *Amanda*. How does that sound?"

I nodded, which meant *yes, yes, and yes*.

She eased me out of the hug. "In that case, I think we better get going. You and Sandra have school, you know."

"Or we could stay home and watch movies all day," I said.

She laughed. "Sorry, but no."

"Or *you and I* could stay home and watch movies all day. We could drop Sandra off first and just not tell her. It would be mother-daughter bonding time."

"Oh, would it? And what would Ty do?"

"Um . . . master the ancient art of Japanese flower arranging?"

"I don't think so."

"Take a nap?"

She laughed again. "Get up, you goofy girl and go tell your brother and sister it's time to go. I'm just going to pop quickly into the bathroom."

Of course she was going to pop quickly into the bathroom, because she popped quickly into the bathroom before we went *any*where. Because she was Mom. *My* mom. And it wouldn't be a quick pop, but a medium pop. Daughters knew these things about their mothers.

"Fine," I said. "But don't stay in there forever, lady."

I stood up, and I felt so light and happy that I dashed to the kitchen and slid in on my sock feet.

"I'm *baaaaack*!" I announced. "And it's time to go, so get up, you lazy bums!"

Ty giggled. I touched the tip of his nose and said, *"Beeeeep!"*

Sandra, I ignored. Except not really, because how could I? I could sense her presence whether I wanted to or not.

"Sorry, Winnie," she mumbled.

I allowed myself to look at her, and there she was: my big sister who was sometimes annoying, but more often funny. Who said it was okay to be weird. Who apologized on her own without waiting for Mom to make her.

Just like that, I liked her again, and in my head, *I* said sorry to her for wishing (even for a second) that she wasn't my sister.

"Good, because you should be," I said. I went ahead and grinned. "And . . . apology accepted."

May

M Y MOM'S SISTER, Aunt Lucy, was my favorite aunt in the universe. Not because she was my *only* aunt, either. She was my favorite aunt not just in *my* universe, but in the entire universe of *all* aunts, everywhere.

Why?

I made a list:

The first reason was because she was pretty. "Pretty Aunt Lucy," we called her, because that's what Sandra had called her when she was little. Sandra had been confused about who was coming to visit one Thanksgiving, never mind that we had just the one aunt Lucy, and she said to Mom, "You mean *pretty* Aunt Lucy? That one?"

Maybe the name wouldn't have stuck if Aunt Lucy had a zillion moles and each mole had a zillion hairs sticking out of it. Mrs. Lumpkin, who taught third grade, had a mole like that. It was on her cheek, and Amanda and I named it "Lumpy." We didn't call it that out loud, though. We never ran up to Mrs. Lumpkin on the playground and waved at her mole, saying, "Hi there, Lumpy! How's life, Lumpy?"

But Aunt Lucy did not have a single mole that I knew of. She *did* have long, glossy, brown hair and a happy smile, and Amanda said she was really good at makeup. I wouldn't know. I wasn't a makeup kind of girl. But when Amanda met Aunt Lucy last Christmas, she pulled me aside and whispered, "Omigosh, is your aunt a model?"

"No," I said.

"She could be," Amanda said.

"Okay, but she's not."

"But she *could* be. Omigosh, did you notice the silver sparkles on her eyelashes? I totally want to have sparkly eyelashes when I'm a grown-up!"

The second reason Aunt Lucy was my favorite aunt was that despite being a grown-up, she wasn't old and wrinkly and boring. She was young and not yet married, so she spoiled me, Sandra, and Ty rotten whenever she visited. She took us to the movies and bought us kids' packs with popcorn, candy, and Coke, and she didn't make us substitute a juice box. She didn't even lecture us about caffeine!

The third and last and *best* reason that Aunt Lucy was my favorite aunt was because she had a friend from college who lived in New York City! And her friend asked if Aunt Lucy would take care of her apartment while she was traveling for a job-thing, and Aunt Lucy said yes, and she invited Sandra and me to come and stay with her for an entire weekend!

IN NEW YORK CITY! *THE REAL NEW YORK CITY! AND MOM AND DAD SAID YES AND BOUGHT US PLANE TICKETS AND A DRESSY OUTFIT APIECE, IN CASE WE POSSIBLY ENDED UP GOING TO THE THEATER!!!*

And now—it was incredible—here I was, zooming through the skies on my way to the Big Apple. Right now the other fourth graders at Trinity were singing "Kumbaya" in music class, but not me. I was too busy flying to New York with my sister for an entire long weekend!!!

Amanda wanted me to bring her an "I ♥ New York" shirt. Chantelle wanted me to get her a famous person's signature.

I said, "Like whose?" And she said, "Anybody's! Or wait, I know. Al Roker's, from the *Today* show!"

I didn't know who Al Roker was, or even what that show was, so Chantelle explained that it was a talk show her mom loved.

I said, "Okay, I'll try," and my teacher jumped in and said that in that case, would I also get the autograph of another handsome man from that same show?

"Okay, I'll try," I said again, but now I felt bad because I'd forgotten the second man's name. Oh, well. It probably wouldn't matter, because Mom said I probably wouldn't see either of the two handsome men. She gave an entire speech about it, explaining that yes, there were a lot of famous people in New York, but that Sandra and I needed to remember several things:

First, famous people were people just like us, only famous, and we shouldn't be overly starstruck.

Second, even though New York was full of famous people, we shouldn't expect them to pop up everywhere like Whac-A-Mole moles. (Actually, I added the "Whac-A-Mole" part.)

And third, she wouldn't mind having Al Roker's autograph herself, or the autograph of the man whose name I'd forgotten. She wasn't picky.

I hoped I did see someone famous, because what if I really did come home with famous people's signatures? What if I came home with ten or twenty or thirty famous people's signatures? Think how amazed everybody would be! From then on *I* would be famous, pretty much!

I got so excited that I had to fan myself with my ticket, and Sandra had to tell me to stop.

"Winnie, I mean it," Sandra said, because it wasn't the first time she'd asked. *"Quit."*

"Sorry. Sorry!" I needed to remember to be nice to Sandra, because without her, I wouldn't be here. There was no way Mom would have let me fly on my own, even though I'd have been fine with it. Even though I *did* accidentally forget I had two quarters in my pocket, and when I went through security, the beeper went off and two security guards had to pull me aside and they scanned me with a special metal detector wand.

Sandra was mortified. I thought it was awesome. It's possible I would have found it less awesome if Sandra hadn't been with me, however.

Over the airplane's intercom, the flight attendant announced that we'd reached our cruising altitude and we could now use laptops or iPods if we wanted. Sandra didn't have an iPod, but she plugged her headphones into the jack on her armrest and slipped them over her ears.

I poked her and asked, "What are you listening to?"

She held one earpiece away from her head. "Huh?"

"What are you listening to?"

"Music. Shush." She dropped the earpiece back in place and closed her eyes.

I stuck out my tongue. Then I poked her again.

"What?" she said, her eyes flying open.

I waved. "Hi!"

"Hello, and now *good-bye.* Look out the window. Read your book. Do whatever you want, but let me take a nap. *Please?"*

Well, hmmph, I thought. I couldn't believe we were on a plane and she wanted to nap. What was wrong with that girl?

I looked out the window. All I could see were clouds. No earth. Certainly no Atlanta, though I knew it was down there. It didn't disappear just because I wasn't there. It wasn't like playing peekaboo with Ty when he was a baby, when he thought I could make a yellow rubber ducky vanish entirely—as in, gone—just by hiding it from his sight.

Wouldn't it be weird if things *did* disappear the moment you stopped looking at them? If the world only existed when you were around to see and smell and touch and feel and taste it?

If that was the case, did that mean I didn't exist to Sandra, since her eyes were shut?

I poked her again. Her eyes flew open, and I smiled my cutest smile. *Why, look! It's me!!* I hoped my smile said. *Your darling sister!*

"Winnie, you are driving me crazy," she said through gritted teeth.

I patted her head and said, "You can go to sleep now. I won't bug you anymore."

She didn't look convinced, but she once more closed her eyes.

As for me, I stayed true to my word. Yes, I was flying through the air with the great big world all around me, and yes, I felt tiny, but I also felt . . . mighty. The world wasn't going anywhere, and neither was I, because how could I? Here I was already.

We landed in New York at five o'clock. The airport was crowded and dirty, and Sandra made me hold her hand as we pushed a path through all the people. She said she didn't want to lose me, but I think she didn't want *me* to lose *her*. Yes, Sandra was my big sister, but guess what? Sometimes she needed me just as much as I needed her.

When we got to baggage claim, we were faced with a milling group of people wearing suits and brimmed caps, all of them holding up signs with people's names on them. One said "Mr. Yamasuto," and another said "Continental World Explorers."

"Who are these people?" I asked.

"Limo drivers," Sandra told me.

"Whoa. Are we taking a limo?"

"I wouldn't count on it," Sandra said.

I didn't mind. It was thrilling enough just to soak in how *different* everybody in New York was. All sorts of people lived in Atlanta, like white people and black people and Hispanic people and people who were Asian. But the two biggest groups were white people and black people, for sure.

Here, I couldn't pick out a "biggest" group. It was a total mix. I saw one man wearing a tall black hat and a long black coat, and along with a thick beard, he had long curls that hung down in front of his ears. Near him, I saw an Indian woman with a jewel in the middle of her forehead. She was wearing a silky dress that reached the floor, and her little girl was wearing one just like it. I saw Muslim women wearing head scarves and white people with dreadlocks. I saw three tall, gangly guys with dark skin, white teeth, and big smiles. One of them made a peace sign at me, and I grinned and made a peace sign back.

Then I spotted Pretty Aunt Lucy. Like the limo drivers, she was holding up a sign. It said, "The Perry Girls!" She'd decorated it with gold and silver star stickers.

"Aunt Lucy!" I called, waving like a maniac. Her eyes landed on us, and she rushed over and hugged us tight.

"You're here!" she exclaimed. "You're really here!"

"I know!" I cried.

"We're actually in *New York*," Sandra said, and for once she wasn't being sarcastic. She was just as in awe as I was. "I can't believe it."

"Well, let's get out of this smelly airport and get you two some dinner," Aunt Lucy said. "You girls like pizza, right?"

We nodded.

"Great, because New York is famous for its pizza." She took my travel suitcase and pulled it for me. Sandra and I followed her through the maze of sights and smells, including a poster of a hungry-looking baby with the words No CHILD SHOULD GO WITHOUT.

Aunt Lucy caught me reading it and stopped so abruptly that I bonked into her.

"*Ack.* Sorry!" I said, but she said, "No, no. My fault. It's just . . . that billboard . . . I guess I should warn you that you might see some homeless people while you're here."

"We might?" I said.

"Actually, you *definitely* will, and I'm so sorry. It's *awful.*

It's terrible and depressing . . . but you get used to it." Her brow wrinkled. "Actually, you don't. Or at least, I haven't."

She looked so worried that I took her hand. I didn't know what to say, so I just gave her a small smile.

She managed to smile back. "Well . . . we'll just do the best we can, right?"

"Right," I said.

We reached the airport exit and stepped into the warm outside air. Almost everyone seemed to be smoking, and I thought, *Whoa, lung cancer city*. There was a lot of litter, too. I saw a guy flick the butt of his cigarette plainly onto the sidewalk, and I considered going over and reminding him to be nice to Mother Earth.

I took a step in his direction, but Aunt Lucy said, "This way, Winnie," and steered me to the back of a long line of people waiting to get a taxi. A woman in a blue outfit like one a cop might wear was moving down the line saying, "Destination? Destination?"

She wouldn't reach us for a minute or two.

"Can we go to the top of the Empire State Building?" I asked.

"Sure," Aunt Lucy said.

"What about the Statue of Liberty?" Sandra said.

"If you want. I've heard it takes about three hours to get in, though."

"Three hours?" Sandra repeated.

"Or we can take a ferry and look at it from the harbor.

We don't have to decide this very second." The uniformed taxi lady reached us, and Aunt Lucy said, "Central Park South." She said it like she was a woman of the world. I was impressed.

The taxi lady ripped off a stub of paper and handed it to Aunt Lucy, saying, "Number twenty-two."

I headed toward the end of the line of taxis, because that's what I'd seen the other people do. The taxi lady grabbed my shoulder and turned me around.

"I *said* number twenty-two," she said. "Clean your ears out, girl."

"We go this way," Aunt Lucy told me, and I trotted behind her to a different line of cabs.

"Did that lady tell me to clean my ears out?" I said.

"She did," Sandra marveled. In Atlanta, people didn't randomly tell you to clean your ears out.

Aunt Lucy laughed. "Welcome to New York."

Aunt Lucy's friend's apartment was the size of my entire bedroom, although it was split into different sections. But Aunt Lucy said apartments were hard to come by in New York, and that Catherine—that was her friend—felt lucky to have found hers, because "it was in such a great location."

I didn't know what made the location so great. I wasn't suggesting it was *un*-great. I just didn't know how to tell it apart from what I'd seen on the cab drive from the airport. Looking out the window, all I saw were streets and cars and taxis and a hundred thousand people at least. Some looked like businessmen and -women, others looked a lot less fancy. Like, there were moms pushing babies in strollers and chubby men wearing baseball caps and plain old normal kids, too. There were even kids my age walking along alone, going wherever they were going.

There wasn't much to do in the apartment, since it was so small. So we dropped off our suitcases and headed back out, this time on foot. My head spun from trying to take in all the sights, and then I saw something that made it spin right off my head stalk, practically. I saw a man with crazy white hair that looked like a bird's nest, *and in that bird's nest of hair was an actual parrot!*

A live parrot was living in the man's hair!

"Winnie, stop gawking," Aunt Lucy said, because without realizing it, I'd stopped stock-still in the middle of the sidewalk. I couldn't help it! There was a man in front of me with a parrot in his hair!

"Yeah, and close your mouth before a bee flies in," Sandra said. "Or somebody's cigarette."

"But, Sandra! That man! He had a—"

"Bird in his hair," she finished. "I saw."

"But—"

"But what? You act like you've never seen a man with a bird in his hair before."

"I haven't." I frowned. "Have *you*?"

She dropped her *nothing shocks me, not even a bird in a nest made of hair* act. "Are you crazy, you crazy girl?!" she exclaimed, thwonking my head. "Winnie! That man had a *bird* in his hair!"

One sad thing was that Aunt Lucy was right about there being homeless people. On the way to the pizza place, I saw a man holding a tin can with a taped-on piece of paper that said, *Help a vet.*

I still had my two quarters from the airport, which the airport guard had given back to me once he decided I wasn't a threat to national security, so I dropped them in his can.

"God bless you, angel," he said.

"Um, God bless you, too," I said.

After our pizza—which *was* delicious, and which we folded in half before eating, because Aunt Lucy said that was the way New Yorkers did it—we walked back to the apartment. This time we passed a black woman and her little boy, who looked about Ty's age. The little boy held a hat in his lap, and in the hat were coins and a few bills.

I looked at Aunt Lucy, who smiled and tried to be brave in the face of that distressing sight. She fished a five-dollar bill from her wallet.

"Sandra, do you want to give it to her?" I whispered, since I'd been the one to give the older man my quarters.

Sandra shook her head. She wanted the lady and her

little boy to have the money, I could tell, but the situation made her nervous. Or upset. Or both?

I took the five-dollar bill and put it in the hat, and the mom said, "Thank you, baby."

"You're welcome." I was holding an unopened can of Dr Pepper—I hadn't gotten around to drinking it at dinner—and I had an idea.

"Is your little boy allowed to have Coke?"

"What's that, baby?" the mom said.

"Soda," Aunt Lucy told me. "In New York, Coke is called soda."

I stored the knowledge away and tried again. "Can your son have soda? Is he allowed?"

"Yeah, baby, sure," the mom said.

I offered my Dr Pepper toward the boy, who said, "Why'd you call that a Coke? That's not a Coke. That's a Dr Pepper."

I frowned, because he had a point. I'd never thought about it, but in Atlanta, *we* called all soft drinks Coke, even when they weren't. And I'd thought New Yorkers were the weird ones for calling Coke soda!

"I don't know," I said. "Do you want it?"

"Yeah!" he said, scrambling up. "Thanks!"

It made me happy that a Coke—er, a Dr Pepper—would make his eyes light up like that. But it also made me feel lonely.

Later, when I was supposed to be falling asleep, I

couldn't. I think I was homesick . . . maybe because seeing that mother and her son made me miss Mom?

I missed Dad, too, and Ty and our house and my bedroom, but I missed Mom the most. Even though it was exciting to be here, home seemed awfully far away.

The next day we went to Central Park. I was tired, so Aunt Lucy bought me an espresso, and it was n-a-s-t-y. So she poured it into a much bigger cup, added lots of cream and five packs of sugar, and after that, it was scrumdiddliumptious! And made me talk really-really-fast and do hyper dancing and bounce from foot to foot until finally Sandra said, "Winnie. *Down.*"

She said it like I was a dog, so I got down on my hands and knees in Central Park and started yip-yip-yipping.

"Omigosh," Sandra said, edging away on the bench.

"But she doesn't have a bird in her hair," Aunt Lucy pointed out. "We need to remember that."

Oh! Oh! And later we saw a famous person taking an afternoon stroll, and it was Al Roker! The real live Al Roker from the fancy morning TV show! He was with a pretty girl who we decided was his daughter. I wanted to run over and say hi, but Aunt Lucy said absolutely not, because New Yorkers respected celebrities' privacy.

"But we're not New Yorkers," I said.

"We are today," Aunt Lucy said.

"Can I take a picture of them?"

"No."

"Can I *draw* a picture of them?"

"With what?"

"Well, can I just call out a general *hellooooo*, and if they happen to look over, then they happen to look over?"

"No, Winnie, you may not," Aunt Lucy said. "And please get up off the grass. I'm not giving you any more belly rubs."

When Sandra and Aunt Lucy weren't watching, I went ahead and waved at the girl anyway. Just an itty-bitty, cupped-palm wave. The girl looked confused, but she waved back. My smile stretched wide. I could feel it.

That day and the next, we did tons of fun things with Aunt Lucy, like buying sea salt caramels from a famous *chocolatier* and seeing a musical version of *Mary Poppins* on Broadway and shopping at the Disney store, which had a window display of a huge doll made up entirely of normal-sized dolls.

Out of all of our adventures, however, I had two definite favorites. The first was going to the top of the Empire State Building, which I insisted we do even though Sandra was like, "Oh, we are *such* tourists."

My response to that was, "Why yes, we are. And when people come to Atlanta to visit the World of Coke, guess what? Then *they're* the tourists."

"Who comes to Atlanta to visit the World of Coke?" Sandra asked.

"Lots of people."

"And their names would be . . . ?"

"The people who visit the World of Coke," I retorted. Then I looked at the people in line with us, taking in their fanny packs and their shirts that said *New York* on them. Did real New Yorkers *ever* did go to the top of the Empire State Building?

At the tippy-top there was a glassed-in observation deck. Initially, Sandra, Aunt Lucy, and I clumped together, because it was freaky being up so high, even with walls.

Then I split off and leaned as far over the railing as I could. Down below, I saw little humans going about doing little human things. My eyes skimmed the zillions of cars, and there were just as many yellow taxicabs as normal cars! In Atlanta, I hardly ever saw taxis.

A tour-guide-y person told us some facts about the Empire State Building, but what stuck with me were the tiny ant people, and the tiny ant cars, and how half of those cars were taxis. Not an eighth, not a fourth, but *half* of them were fully yellow.

On Sunday, we went to a hotel called The Plaza. That was my second favorite adventure, because we got to see a famous portrait of an even famouser girl named Eloise. Eloise was famous even though she wasn't alive. She was a character in a children's book, and in the book, she lived at The Plaza, which was why there was a portrait of her there.

The Plaza in the book was super fancy and posh, and

so was The Plaza in real life. It was *so* fancy, even from the outside, that Sandra didn't want to go in.

"I'm wearing jeans!" she protested.

"So?" Aunt Lucy said. "I am, too."

"But yours are dress-up jeans, and plus you're wearing *those*," Sandra said, gesturing at Aunt Lucy's high-heeled sandals. "I just look . . . grubby."

"*I'm* grubbier," I said. I held out my arms and did a twirl. "Do you feel better now?"

Sandra balked. "The doorman won't let us in. He'll say, 'Hey, you grubby people! Get out of here, you grubby people!'"

"Don't be silly," Aunt Lucy said, and she marched right up to the man standing in front of the hotel. His suit was blue with gold trim. His cap had a gold tassel.

"Excuse me," Aunt Lucy said. "These are my nieces, visiting from Atlanta. We were wondering if you've seen Eloise around, by chance."

Sandra turned red. I, however, was delighted, especially when the doorman played along.

"I'm sorry, but she just stepped out," he informed us. "I *could* show you her portrait, if you'd like. Might you be interested in taking a peek?"

"Oh, yes," Aunt Lucy said.

The doorman, whose name tag said FREDDY, led us into the hotel. I twisted my head from side to side, trying to soak it all in. I glanced up to check out the ceiling, and even *it* was impressive.

In a wide hall, Freddy gestured at an oil painting which showed Eloise looking just exactly like she looked in the books Mom used to read me: plump, smug, and awesome in a ruffly white shirt and pleated black skirt.

"I'll tell you a secret if you promise to keep it to yourself," Freddy said, lowering his voice.

I nodded.

"This portrait? It's not the real one."

"What?"

He bent at his waist and spoke into my ear. "The real one got stolen."

My eyes popped. "The real one got *stolen*," I told Sandra and Aunt Lucy.

"By who?" Sandra asked.

"A gang of fraternity boys," Freddy said.

"Really?" Aunt Lucy said.

I jiggled from foot to foot. It was so cool to discover something about New York that Aunt Lucy didn't even know.

"Really," Freddy said. "Fortunately, the artist was kind enough to paint a new one."

"Thank goodness, because think how upset Eloise would be," I said.

"Very true," Freddy said. "When she returns, shall I give her your regards?"

"Yes, please. Tell her that Winnie, Lucy, and Sandra say hi."

Sandra tried to protest.

"Winnie, Lucy, *and* Sandra," I repeated firmly. It struck me all at once that here I was, having a lovely chat with the doorman of The Plaza Hotel in New York City, when just this past Thursday—was it only *three days* ago?—I'd been taking my multiplication test while trying to ignore Alex Plotkin's unsneaky nose-picking.

In the grand scheme of things, three days was nothing . . . and yet three short days ago, I hadn't ridden in a cab, or folded a piece of pizza in half, or given my *soda* to a stranger. I certainly hadn't tried espresso or waved at a famous person's daughter.

Sophistication zinged through every cell of me. It was amazing how much I'd changed in such a short amount of time.

"So you'll give Eloise our regards?" I said.

Freddy bowed formally, taking off his cap and holding it at his waist. "Consider it done."

June

June was not the prettiest name for a month, I thought. It also wasn't the prettiest name for a girl. Or a woman, *or* a man. I didn't know anyone named June, but I'd heard of people being named that. Me? I would never name my kid that, and the same went for Myrtle, Thelma, Phillipa, and Nunchucks. Hee-hee, I just made that one up. I've never heard of anyone named Nunchucks. It would be an awful name, though.

But the word *June* made happiness bubble up in me even though I didn't love the sound of it. Because in Georgia, school ended the first week of June, and that meant summer vacation! And summer vacation meant hot hot hotness—especially in Atlanta, which some people even called *Hot*lanta—and hotness meant . . . swimming pools! Yay!

Next month I was signed up to go to day camp with Amanda, but this month was all about swimming. Half the time I went with Amanda to her neighborhood pool, which had an awesome snack bar but no slide, and the other half of the time, Amanda came with me to Garden Hills Pool, a public pool in my neighborhood. The snack bar at Garden Hills wasn't anything special, but the pool was huge, with a baby-splashing area for Ty, a curlicue slide, and two—count 'em, *two*—diving boards.

Amanda loved going to the pool almost as much as I did, although she did have one very bad habit called Caring Too Much About Her Tan. "Pooey on tans," I said, frequently and loudly. Swimming pools were for *swimming*. That's why they were called *swimming* pools. You didn't hear anyone calling them tanning pools, did you?

Worrying about your "base tan" was just plain silly. If you spend enough time outside, you turn tan. End of story. Unless you were pale-as-a-codfish Dinah Devine, but she was a different story.

Sandra argued that I was a different story, too—an "olive-toned" story—and that I could only be pooey-ish about tans because I, myself, got tan so easily. To that I said, "Pooey again!" But secretly I was proud of myself for turning such a lovely golden brown color, a color that wasn't "olive-toned" at all. *Please.*

One Wednesday morning, Mom took me, Sandra, and Ty to Garden Hills Pool for a pool picnic. For once, it was just us three kids, because Amanda had plans to go shopping with her mom, Chantelle was visiting her cousins—she had oodles of them—and neither Sandra nor Ty had invited a friend.

But it was nice, sometimes, just being with my own family. (Well, minus Dad, since he had to work.) It was summer, we were at the pool, and the sky was crystal blue. I knew it was going to be a great day.

We laid out our towels and got busy having fun. Mom read her book and did not swim, that bad lady, because that was her version of fun. Sandra dog-paddled back and forth in the deep end and pretended not to stare at one particular lifeguard who wasn't even nice, in my opinion. Ty jumped around in the kiddie pool, and when I say "jumped," I mean that he literally *jumped*, flinging himself into the air and coming down hard on his booty, which was no longer padded with a swim diaper like it had been in previous summers. He made epic waves, which not everybody appreciated.

As for me, I spent the bulk of my time working on handstands and flips in the shallow end. I was excellent at handstands. I was getting better at flips. Currently, I could tuck underwater, curl up in a ball, and do four in a row without taking a breath. I had my sights set on ten. (This was for front flips, not backward ones. With backward flips, I could do three.)

We were happy and splashy and yay-summer-vacation-y . . . and then things got interesting, as they *always* did when pools and kids and sunshine were involved. One moment I was underwater, upside down in a land of legs and feet, and my lungs had the nice feeling of being full of air to the point of almost bursting.

Then I rolled forward out of my handstand and popped out of the water, letting my lungs go ahead and burst in a joyful exhalation. I was flushed and proud as I turned to find someone to admire me: Sandra or Mom or Ty, any of them would do.

My own needs went down the drain when I spotted Ty, though. He was standing slack-armed in the kiddie pool, his little-boy belly poking out from above his shark swimming trunks. An innocent bystander might think he had on his stubborn expression, which involved a deeply frowning face and a jutted-out lower lip.

But because I was his big sister, I could see that he was actually wearing his I'm-not-so-happy-right-now-and-I-might-cry-and-so-I-am-covering-it-up-with-stubborness expression. The telltale signs were the tremble in his jutting-out lip and the slight caterpillar-legs wiggle of his sweet eyebrows.

From what I could tell, the reason for his distress was a girl in a hot pink bikini with exploding ruffles. She was about Ty's age, and she was standing in front of Ty and saying something to him. It appeared to be a bossy sort of thing, because she was waggling her finger at him, too.

No, ma'am, Frilly Missy, I thought, hopping out of the big kid pool and marching over. *You do NOT get to steal my brother's fun.*

"What's going on?" I said, splashing into the kiddie pool and putting my arm around my little brother.

Frilly Missy pointed at Ty. "He's wearing pink. Boys aren't allowed to wear pink."

Really? I thought. *You're* really *going to make us go there?*

"What's your name?" I said, cocking my head.

"Erica," she said. She cocked her head right back at me and added a *so there* thrust to her chin. She had been watching *way* too much "big kid" TV. There was no other explanation for such a little girl having such a snotty attitude.

"Well, hello, Erica," I said, behaving especially polite to drive home the message that I was her elder, and she should be treating me with respect. "I'm Winnie, and this is Ty."

Ty hugged my bare leg. He didn't say hello.

"Now, first of all, Ty *isn't* wearing pink," I said, gesturing at Ty's swimming trunks. I didn't want to call her out on not knowing her colors, but the sharks on his suit were blue and gray, and they were baring their teeth against a background of white.

"Is so," Erica said. "On his toes."

I looked at Ty's toes through the kiddie pool water. *Oops.* I'd forgotten that I'd given him a beauty treatment last night, and that it involved painting his toenails. It also involved a karate-chop massage on his back—which made him say *oomph*, that's how manly it was—but, yes, his toes did glisten with Dusky Rose nail polish.

I regrouped. "Okay, fine. Second of all, which I was going to say anyway, boys are so allowed to wear pink. There aren't *rules* about colors."

"Are so."

"Are not."

"Are so."

"Are *not*."

"Are so."

"*Are not!*"

I closed my eyes and put my hand out. *T*, I said silently, privately calling a time-out before my voice got any louder.

Already, mothers were glancing over. Not *Mom* mom, because she'd set herself up in a far-away pool chair and was absorbed in her paperback. Also not Erica's mom, I was guessing, because surely she'd come over if she saw her daughter getting involved in a kiddie pool brawl.

But other moms were giving us the we're-watching-you stares that all moms knew how to do. If things turned ugly, I knew who would be blamed.

"Are so," Erica said despite my traffic-cop hand. I couldn't believe how sure of herself she was even in the presence of someone who was clearly older and wiser. *Are so, are so, are so*, her tone matter-of-fact and almost bored.

I scooped Ty up. "We're done here, Erica. Colors are for everybody, and good-bye. I'm glad we had this little talk."

I turned and sloshed through the shallow water.

"I'm right and you're wrong," she said to my back.

It took all my will to keep sloshing.

"Is she?" Ty asked, once we were a safe distance away.

"What? *No*," I said. "No way."

We reached my blue-and-white striped beach towel, and I bumped him off my hip so that we could both plonk down.

"Hi, kids," Mom said, glancing up from her novel. "Having fun?"

"Of course we are, because we always have fun at the pool," I said. I didn't look at her, but kept my eyes on Ty. He *wasn't* having fun. My job wasn't done if Ty wasn't having fun.

"Oh, good," Mom said. She returned to her novel.

"Can we have money for a snack?" I asked.

"I thought you didn't like the snacks here."

"I don't. Can we?"

"Winnie, I packed lunch for us for this very reason."

"But *Mo-o-o-m*—"

"Oh, fine," she said, obviously more interested in getting back to her book than in arguing with me. She pulled a vinyl pouch from the pool bag, unzipped it, and gave me two dollars. "Chips or popsicles. *No* caffeine."

"Come on," I said, pulling Ty back up to standing. "Thanks, Mom!"

Erica stood in the knee-high water of the kiddie pool, her hands still on her hips. Her head swiveled as she tracked our movements, but we marched past her and paid her no mind. Ty started to, but I squeezed his hand and said, "Eyes straight ahead, buddy. Eyes straight ahead."

We marched past the shallow end of the big pool. We marched past the snack bar.

"Wait," Ty said, trotting to keep up. "We didn't get snacks."

"We might later. That was just so Mom wouldn't ask where we were going."

"Where *are* we going?"

We reached an empty-ish spot of lawn near the deep end of the pool. From here, we had a good view of the slide, the diving board, and the plain old swimming area.

"This'll work," I said. I nodded, then sat down and dangled my feet in the water. I patted the cement next to me. "Sit. Observe. Learn."

He dropped down beside me. He dangled *his* feet in the water. A person flew out of the end of the slide, which was shaped like a tunnel, and the splash made both of us recoil.

"Cool," Ty said.

"Ehh," I said. "I've seen better. I've *done* better."

I scanned the landscape of bodies, bodies, and more bodies, searching for someone who was unusual in one way or another. I had utter confidence I'd succeed. At the pool, if you opened your eyes and didn't just focus on backflips or whatever, there was *always* someone unusual.

Last week, for example, I went into the ladies' changing room to use the bathroom, and I saw a teenager put on a pair of undies that said *Tuesday* across the bottom, even though it was a Friday. I also saw an old lady—like, *Mom's* age—step into a pair of Ariel the Mermaid panties. I knew from going to New York that the Disney store did sell grown-up sizes of princess underwear. But boy, was it strange seeing an actual lady wearing a pair. Plus she had a nose ring. I could *not* imagine Mom with a nose ring. I couldn't imagine Ariel the Mermaid wearing a nose ring, either.

"Okay, here we go," I said to Ty. "Diving board. Second girl in line."

Ty looked over at the diving board. I looked at Ty. His eyebrows went up. "She's got a boy's bathing suit!" He tugged at my arm. "Winnie, that girl has on a boy's bathing suit!"

"They're called *board shorts*," I explained. "But on top, she's wearing a bikini. See?"

"Why?"

"Why a bikini top, but shorts instead of a bikini bottom?" I shrugged. "Maybe she only likes her top half. Maybe she doesn't want people to see her thighs?"

"Why?"

"No idea." I pointed at the part of the pool blocked off for swimming laps. "Now look at the dude practicing his backstroke, the one with all the chest hair."

Ty's head swiveled, his expression open and curious. Then he threw himself against me, hugging my waist.

"I know," I said.

He risked another peek at Chest Hair Man, who was

wearing the type of man's swimsuit that *didn't* look like shorts. I think it was called a Speedo, that type of suit.

Ty whimpered and burrowed back into me.

"I know, I know," I soothed. "Believe me, I know."

"I can see his *mmmfffle*," Ty said into my side.

I giggled—because of the *mmmfffle,* and also because his nose and chin were digging into my ribs. "Can you imagine if Dad wore a bathing suit like that?"

Ty drew back. "He won't, will he? Ever?"

"Not if Mom has anything to do with it," I said. I spotted a new target and spoke quickly. "Ooo, there's a guy walking past us wearing superlong swim trunks. See him? Do you see his fingernails?"

"They're black," Ty marveled.

"Uh-huh, because sometimes boys *do* paint their nails."

"*And* their toenails?"

"If they want to," I said.

Ty flexed his feet, lifting his chubby toes out of the water and admiring them. "Pink is better than black."

"Thinks *you*," I pointed out. "But that guy likes black better, apparently." The guy was far enough away from us that I could use my normal voice again. "You're right, though. Black is more for zombie-hunting, not for going swimming on a beautiful summer day."

My shoulders were growing toasty in the sun. Right now the heat felt good, but I knew how quickly that could change. I leaned back on my palms, pulled my feet out of the

water, and pushed myself into a standing position as grace-
fully as I could, tricky to do without scooching my fanny
on the rough concrete. But fanny-scooching was death to a
bathing suit, as I knew from experience.

Well, fanny-schooching was death to the sort of standard-
issue girl's bathing suit *I* was wearing. My suit was a blue
one-piece, and it was in great condition, without any nubbly
spots or loose elastic. But it was only June. By August, who
knew what state it would be in?

I glanced around for the board-shorts girl. She was sitting
on the opposite side of the pool, chatting with a cute boy and
swishing her feet in the water. *Swish, swish, swish*, not seem-
ing the slightest bit concerned by what all that swishing
might be doing in terms of bathing suit damage.

Maybe that's why she wears board shorts, I thought. *So she
doesn't have to worry about ripping her suit.*

The boy laughed, and something glinted in his ear. It
was an earring. The girl wasn't wearing jewelry, but he was.
I smiled.

"Come on, buddy," I said, reaching out and pulling
Ty up.

A large lady walked past us. Ty followed her with his
gaze, and this time he beckoned for me to lean in.

"She has a mole, and it is *vehwee, vehwee* big," he whispered.

I looked.

"It sure is," I whispered back.

"It's not her fault, though."

"No, moles aren't anyone's fault."

"Do I have any moles?"

"Not yet, although you might grow some. Especially if you eat too many Sour Skittles."

His eyes widened, then narrowed. "Nuh-uh. You just want my Sour Skittles. But guess what? I don't even have any Sour Skittles!"

I still had the two dollars Mom gave me, and I displayed them to Ty. "Snack bar?"

His face lit up. Then he frowned. "But—"

I was way ahead of him. "We'll tell Mom they were out of popsicles—which they are." I didn't know that, but I didn't *not* know that, either. It was summer. Freezers broke, popsicles melted.

I kept hold of Ty's hand as we strolled to the snack bar. "So let's review what we've learned. What do you think that frilly Erica girl would have said about the girl wearing board shorts?"

"That she wasn't allowed?"

"Yup. What about the man in the Speedo?"

"What's a Speedo?"

"The man whose bathing suit was like the bottom half of a bikini," I clarified.

"Um . . . not allowed?"

"Correct again." I squeezed his hand. "So is Erica right about things, and I'm wrong? Or am *I* right, and she's wrong?"

"You're right, and so am I, and she is a poo-poo-head," Ty said. "After we have our snack, will you play in the little kids' pool with me?"

"Absolutely. You can be a dolphin, and I'll be your trainer, and if you do your tricks right, I'll reward you with Skittles."

"Only we'll say they're fish," he said. We got into line at the snack bar. "And if we see that mean Ewica, then she can just . . . just . . ."

"Fluff the ruffles on her bathing suit?"

He grinned. "Yeah!"

His Dusty Rose toenails sparkled in the sunshine, calling to mind seashells and dolphin treats and all things summery, splashy, and fun-with-a-capital-*fuh*.

July

I was so mad at Amanda that I could cry. My tears would be as hot as the hot Georgia sun, and I would collect them in a jar and . . . do *something* with them. Pour them on Amanda's head, maybe, so her beautiful blond hair would burn to a frizzle.

Only I would never do that, so fine.

Instead, I kicked Bearie, my stuffed animal bear that I loved. *Ow*. That Bearie was a Very Heavy Bear. He was stuffed with rice, was why, and if the urge fell upon me, I could microwave him and he would get toasty-warm and extra-cuddly. In the winter, I shoved him under the sheets to the bottom of my bed, and he kept my feet cozy while I slept.

Today he made my foot *un*happy, that bad bear. Except it wasn't his fault, since I was the one who kicked him, and that was mean of me, too. It made my heart unhappy.

I scooped him up and clutched him to my chest. "I'm sorry, Bearie," I said. My voice wobbled, and I was tempted to go get a hand mirror so I could watch myself be sad.

Then I remembered that I wasn't sad. I was *mad*, and not at Bearie, but at Amanda.

"Winnie, get down here *now*," Mom called from the foot of the staircase. She was exasperated with me for being draggy and slow on the first day of summer camp. But guess what? I was exasperated, too.

"I can't find my boots," I complained.

"They're *in your closet*. I put them there on purpose."

Perhaps she did, but after I tried them on last night, I kicked them off on purpose. They'd arced through the air and landed humble-jumble by my beanbag chair, but I chose not to acknowledge their existence.

"Grab them and come on," Mom called. She and I were the only ones in the house, as Sandra was with Ty at the park and Dad was at work.

I didn't grab them. I didn't do anything.

"All right," Mom said. I heard the jangle of keys. "I'm leaving. I hope you decide to come with me, because otherwise, you're on your own."

"Fine," I said.

"And I'll be taking the cost of the nonrefundable camp tuition out of your bank account," she added. "The camp that you *begged* me to sign you up for, I might add!"

I heard her open the back door. I heard her shut the back door. Then I heard nothing.

"Oh, mustard," I cursed, scrambling for my boots. "Wait! I'm coming, sheesh!"

I sat in the backseat of the car even though I was allowed to sit up front when Sandra wasn't along.

But today I didn't want to. Today I fastened my seat belt, tucked my legs beneath me, and curled up next to the door. I wished I were anywhere but here, being forced to go to Wilderness Survival Camp ALL BY MYSELF for an entire week. It wasn't sleepover camp, so I'd get to go home at the end of each day. But, still. Mom didn't understand that the only reason I'd begged to be signed up was because Amanda and I would be going to camp *together*. Surviving in the woods? Eating hot dogs and possibly even worms, if we ran out of food and it was either eat worms or starve? What could be more awesome?

Then Amanda backed out, and her mom, unlike mine, said, "Sure, honey, go right ahead." And why? So she could go to *cheerleading* camp instead! *Grrrr*.

"Winnie, you're going to be fine," Mom said when we pulled up to the camp drop-off. We'd ridden in silence, me with my arms crossed over my chest the whole time and my head turned determinedly away. "You're going to be more than fine. You're going to have *fun*, honey."

"No," I said. "Not without Amanda."

Mom laughed, which made me even madder. She was laughing at my pain!

"You don't even care, do you?" I said.

"Winnie," Mom said, unbuckling and twisting in her seat. She put her hand on my leg. I jerked away. She stretched farther and put her hand on my leg again, and, so, fine. I left it there.

"I do care, and I'm sorry I laughed. I wasn't laughing at you, though."

"Oh, were you laughing *with* me?" I said sarcastically. "I wasn't laughing, in case you didn't notice."

She squeezed my knee. "Let me try again. Maybe I was laughing at you, but I didn't mean to hurt your feelings, and if I did, I apologize. I was laughing because Winnie, you make friends more easily than anyone I've ever met."

I sideways-looked at her. "I do?"

"You don't need Amanda to have a good time," she said. "Amanda is wonderful. I love Amanda."

"So do I," I said.

"But her dropping out of camp shouldn't ruin it for you. And I know it won't—that's why I laughed."

I glowered at her, but it was a somewhat less glowery glower than it could have been. It was a glower that meant *Hmmph. I* might *forgive you, but only because I'm so nice.*

"What if no one talks to me?" I said.

"Then you talk to them," she said. She didn't laugh, choosing this time to tease me by being overly serious. "Now, I *know* being chatty is hard for you—"

"*Mo-o-o-m.*"

"And I know you're very shy—"

"*Mo-o-o-m!*"

"But just try, sweetie. And if, for whatever reason, you

can't get past your paralyzing fear of telling jokes, being silly, and doing monkey impressions—"

"I don't do monkey impressions," I said, giggling despite myself. Then I mooed, and I sounded exactly like a cow, because I *did* do an excellent cow impression. "That's the interrupting *cow*, Mom. Sheesh."

"Right. Of course. But my point is the same: If you find yourself without any cows to interrupt—"

I rolled my eyes.

"—then fake it till you make it. That's all."

"Sure, sure. *That's* all. Easy for you to say."

"You're going to do great. I have complete and udder faith in you."

"Did you just say you had *udder* faith in me?"

She smiled. "You inherited that charm and wit from someone, you know."

"You mean Dad? Dad's not charming and witty. He's just weird."

"Bye, Winnie," she said, chuckling. She gave me a final knee squeeze. "I'll see you at three, and you can tell me all the fabulous things you did."

By lunchtime, I had yet to reach a verdict, as the only semi-fabulous thing that had happened so far was getting to take off our shoes and tromp around in the river, looking for good skipping stones. Yes, that was fun, but was it *fabulous*? I wasn't yet ready to go that far.

I guess being here wasn't horrible, though. The counselors were nice enough. One was named Jake and the other was named Lily, and they told us they were both in college studying to be forest rangers. They didn't seem like the type of people to pick favorites or be randomly mean to kids, which was good.

They were very excited about leaves and bark and animal droppings, and I heard one girl camper whisper to her friend that they were "nature geeks," but I didn't mind that one bit. In fact, I thought it said more—in a bad way—about the whispering girl than it did about Jake and Lily. Ever since I was Ty's age, Sandra had drilled into me that being geeky was definitely better than being snobby.

"Plus, you can be geeky *and* still be cool," Sandra had often pointed out. "If you're a snob, you're a snob, and snobs are stupid."

So the counselors were cool, and so was the schedule of activities they'd planned for us. Like, tomorrow we were going to break open owl droppings and see what was inside. I'd have to wait and see, but that might qualify as fabulous.

The camp itself was cool, too, I suppose. It was at the Chattahoochee Nature Center, so there was *lots* of nature around. If Ty was here, he'd be cramming rocks and feathers and sticks into his pockets like crazy. Then, when he got home, Mom would grab him before he entered the house and say, "Whoa, buddy. Nature stays outside."

Thinking about Ty made me lonely, though—and also

pointed a big blinky arrow at the one part of camp I didn't like. Without Amanda here, I didn't know a single soul. I'd *possibly* seen one of the girl campers at Garden Hills Pool, but I wasn't sure. Either way, I'd never officially met her.

If Mom was here, she'd tell me to skip over and say, "Why, hi there! Do you have a red polka-dotted one-piece, and do you wear a nose plug when you swim?"

But I didn't, and anyway, Polka Dot had plenty of friends already, so she didn't need me. There were eleven kids in the survival camp—six boys and five girls—and Polka Dot was part of a foursome made up of all the girls but me. The four of them clearly knew each other outside of camp, which I deduced from multiple clues:

All four girls wore matching ensembles: cute shorts, white T-shirts knotted at the small of their backs, white tube socks pulled up to their knees, and sneakers of a matching-ish variety. Meaning, their sneakers weren't identical, but they were certainly in the same shoe family. Me? I had on my hand-me-down hiking boots from Sandra.

Also, all four girls thought bugs were gross and said *ewwww* when Jake showed them a grasshopper in his cupped hand.

Also times two, they were all obsessed with some boy who worked at Starbucks, and they talked about him almost constantly. I'd learned already that he was *gorrrrrgeous*, that he played the guitar, that he was "emo, but not really," and that he had a girlfriend who didn't deserve him. I even knew his name, which was Ian. I knew Ian's name, and yet I hadn't managed to nail down the girls' names, because they didn't call each other by their names. Instead, they went by "Silly" and "Spaz" and "Bootylicious" and "Sugar Booger."

Personally, I would not want to be called "Sugar Booger." I would not want to be called "Bootylicious," either. In fact I highly disapproved of anyone—especially a girl my age!— being called "Bootylicious."

So in my head, I thought of them as the Polka Dots. The Polka Dots went EVERYWHERE with their arms linked, even the narrow nature trails, and even when it meant bumping into low-hanging branches.

And behind them? Me. I was the cheese, like in "The Farmer in the Dell." I found myself humming it all day long. The humming was out loud, but I sang the words silently, and only to myself. *The cheese stands alone. The cheese stands alone. Hi-ho the derry-o, the cheese stands alone!*

Day two of Wilderness Survival Camp was a repeat of day one, except with different activities. The best activity was learning how to make a fire—and I admit it, that part was fabulous. At home, we made a fire by turning on our fireplace. With a switch. The logs weren't real and neither were the flames. They were made of gas, and at the bottom, they were blue.

But Jake and Lily taught us how to start a real fire. First they split us up into groups of three, and my group consisted of me, one of the Polka Dots, and a boy named Connor. The Polka Dot in my group sighed a lot and looked yearningly at the other Polka Dots. Basically, she was boring.

Connor was nice, though. He had long hair—the longest hair I'd ever seen on a boy my age—and he was good at listening to directions. While the Polka Dot sighed, Connor and I did everything Jake and Lily told us to.

First we gathered some dry moss and broke it into pieces. That would be our "tinder," Lily told us. Then we collected lots of different sized sticks. We used the smallest sticks to build a teepee around the moss, and then, with Lily right nearby in case of a forest fire, Connor struck a match and poked it onto the pile of moss.

The moss caught on fire *like that*. It was awesome! You couldn't have a fire made *only* out of moss, because the moss burned too quickly, but the flames lasted just long enough to catch the small sticks on fire.

"Sweet," Lily said. "See how the sticks on the outside fall inward to feed the fire? Now start adding bigger sticks. *Perfect*, you two. You're naturals!"

Connor and I grinned at each other. His face was flushed, and his long hair had grown sweaty, but I didn't care. Anyway, my hair probably looked sweaty, too.

The Polka-Dot member of our group wasn't sweaty or

dirty at all, and her hair was still in its perky updo, decorated with about fifty clippies. But she didn't know how to build a fire, now did she?

On Wednesday morning, I didn't complain when it was time to head off for camp. In fact, I was ready before Mom was.

"So you *are* having fun, huh?" Mom said.

"No comment," I said cheerfully.

She smiled and kissed the top of my head. "I'm proud of you, sweetie. I knew you'd make it work."

That day, we hiked to a place called the Raptor Center. A volunteer gave us a tour and told us it was a hospital for birds of prey that'd been wounded. She showed us a falcon with a broken leg, a hawk missing a chunk of her wing because someone shot her, and a bald eagle that landed on a power line and got slightly electrocuted.

"Poor thing," I said.

"Yeah," Connor said. "How's an eagle supposed to know what a power line is?"

He and I talked the whole way back from the Raptor Center, mostly about animals. Connor said he was an animal rights activist, which I didn't know kids *could* be.

"Sure they can," he said. "It just means you care about animals and don't think people should do cruel experiments on them."

"Oh. Then I'm an animal activist, too."

"Cool," he said, holding out his fist. I touched my knuckles to his and giggled.

"Do you have any pets?" I asked.

"A dog," he said. "She only has three legs, because before we got her, someone tied a lit firecracker to her tail."

"And it blew off her *leg*?"

"She's fine, though. She can still run around and play fetch and stuff."

"What's her name?" I asked.

"Lucky," he said.

I laughed without thinking. Then I clapped my hand over my mouth. "Omigosh. *Omigosh*, I'm *so* sorry."

"No, it's okay. She didn't die, so she is lucky."

"Plus she gets to live with you, so there's one more reason."

He smiled and kicked the dirt trail.

Ahead of us, the Polka Dots launched into a Rockettes routine. Earlier in the week I might have thought something like, *Ugh, really? A high-kicking routine at Wildnerness Survival Camp? Why, in case a bear comes along and you need to kick it in the nose?*

But they looked like they were enjoying themselves, so I didn't.

If a bear did amble out of the woods, however, I would not leave my life in the hands—or high-kicking feet—of the Polka Dots. Nope, I'd climb a tree and yell for Connor to fol-

low me. We'd pelt the bear with pinecones, and if that didn't
work, we'd both be interrupting cows and moo as loudly
as we could, until the bear fainted dead away out of pure
confusion.

Imagining the two of us mooing from up in a tree made
me giggle.

"What?" Connor said.

"Nothing," I said. "But I do have a joke for you. Wanna
hear it?"

"Okay."

"Knock, knock," I said.

"Who's there?"

"Interrupting cow."

"Interrupting cow—"

I interrupted him, of course. *"MOOOOO!"*

On Thursday, we went canoeing in the Chattahoochee
River, and Connor and I shared a canoe. He kept splashing
me, so I splashed him back, and we both ended up drenched.

On Friday, we did a community service project, which
was to clean up trash from a nearby public park.

The Polka Dots didn't like this, and they turned into
Grumpy Dots.

"We shouldn't have to pay to do chores," complained
the girl I might or might not have seen at Garden Hills Pool.
"Especially on our last day of camp."

"Yeah," the others chorused.

I felt sad for a second, thinking about how it really was the last day. Once camp was over, I'd never see Connor again—not unless we ended up going to the same college, or if we randomly ran into each other at Baskin-Robbins, say.

Then I shook that gloomy thought away. The fact that it was our last day meant we should enjoy it, not be gloomy or grumpy about it.

"Come on, you guys," I said to the Polka Dots. "It won't be that bad. Plus, we'll be doing something good for the earth."

"Wh-hoo," the shortest Polka Dot said sourly.

"Well, *I* think it'll be fun," I said, and I wasn't just saying it. I was excited because we'd been given special tools to use called Trash Gators. They were long poles with a handle at one end and a snapping mouth at the other end. If you squeezed the handle, the mouth would clamp down on whatever you wanted to pick up: beer cans, potato-chip bags, anything!

I headed off toward Connor, squeezing the handle of my Trash Gator experimentally.

The Garden Hills Polka Dot grabbed my arm and said, "Wait a sec. We have a question for you."

I turned back. All four Polka Dots gathered close.

"Do you like that boy?" one of them asked.

I furrowed my brow. "Who? *Connor?*"

"Yeah," the Polka Dot from my fire-making group said. "Do you think he's cute?"

Well, huh. I guess I did, but I saw no reason to share this with the Dots. "He's okay."

"But do you like him?" the Garden Hills Dot pressed. "Like, *like* him like him?"

"We're just friends," I said, because I hadn't reached the boy-crazy stage yet. I knew girls who had—for example, the Polka Dots with their Starbucks crush—but not me.

The Dots looked disappointed.

The shortest Dot stepped closer and said, "Well, we think his friend is *totally* crush-worthy." She used her chin to indicate a boy wearing a Braves ball cap. "Don't you?"

I glanced at the boy she meant. I hadn't said a word to him the whole week—well, other than *thanks* when he handed me a crayon I needed. We'd been doing leaf rubbings. He had the burnt sienna, which had always been one of my favorite crayons.

"Isn't he adorable?" Short Dot said.

"*So* adorable," Fire-Making Dot said.

"We call him Mars Bar," the roundest of the Dots said, making all the Dots giggle.

"*Mars Bar?*" I said. "Why?"

"Because we aren't sure what his real name is," Short Dot explained.

"Ahhh," I said. "But why Mars Bar?"

"Because Mars Bars are yummy," Garden Hills Dot said, which led to more giggling. "And because his name is something like that."

"Something like *Mars Bar*?" What name sounded something like Mars Bar?!

"Not the *whole* Mars Bar," Short Dot said. "Just the Mars part."

Round Dot nodded. "Yeah. It's like *Nars*, or *Sarge*, or something."

"Maybe it's Plars," Fire-Making Dot said.

Plars, I thought, my lips twitching. Maybe the Dots weren't as bad as I'd thought.

"Or Jarz," I suggested. "With a *z*."

"Well, of course with a *z*," Fire-Making Dot said. "What other way is there?"

"Girls!" Lily called. "More trash collecting, less gabbing!"

"Coming!" I called back. Again I started off, and again Garden Hills Dot stopped me.

"If you find out his name, will you tell us?" she asked.

I grinned at them. "Sure."

Connor and I had a blast picking up litter. We made up a game we called Gator Grab, which involved grabbing aluminum cans and using our Trash Gators to try and toss them into the park's recycling bins. It would have been easier to walk over and drop the cans into the bins, but it was more fun to try to lob them in from several yards away.

It took finesse, it took precision, and it took excellent timing, skills that neither Connor nor I possessed. One of Connor's cans flew so high that I cried out, "Aaah! You're going to hit a little birdie! Fly, little birdie! Fly for your life!" Another time, I released the handle grip too late, and the Coke can went sailing *behind* me and clonked our counselor Jake on the head.

I cringed. "Sorry!"

Jake rubbed his head. Connor cracked up. I did, too, once Jake wasn't looking.

As for Mars Bar, I did make a stab at finding out his name. I didn't want to ask Connor, because that would have been weird, and what if Connor thought *I* had a crush on him? Which I didn't, of course, but the thing about crushes was that once somebody—*any*body—mentioned them, the whole subject became . . . like . . . explosive.

I didn't want Mars Bar *or* Connor exploding on me, so I played it cool. I strolled toward Mars Bar with the thought of saying, "Hey, I'm Winnie. It's the last day of camp, and I still don't know what your name is. Isn't that weird?"

But I totally blew it. I said, "Hey, I'm—" And then I froze! *I totally froze!*

I froze because the Dots were right. Whatever his name was, he was adorable. His brown hair curled up from beneath his Braves hat, and his hazel eyes glinted in the sun.

But he was more than just adorable. He was . . .

Well, I guess *one* way to describe him was . . .

Ag. I had never had this happen to me, and certainly not with a boy. But there I stood like a frozen corn dog until he broke the silence, saying, "Hey back. And you're what?"

I wiggled my jaw and got it to work. "Huh?"

"You said, 'Hey, I'm . . .'" He circled his hand. "But you didn't finish. So, what are you?"

I stared at him. I didn't know what I was. It was the strangest thing.

Mars Bar smiled, but he was clearly perplexed. He tugged at his ear.

"I'm . . . um . . . picking up trash!" I said. "Yes! Yay, trash!" At Mars Bars' feet lay a piece of crumpled newspaper, and I aimed my Trash Gator at it. I came away with a chunk of the lawn. Clumps of dirt fell on my boot.

"Okay!" I chirped. "Bye now!" I spun on my heel and took my hunk of grass to the Dumpster, where I rose onto my tiptoes and dropped it in. Only I missed, and dirt and grass rained down all over me. *Oh my goodness gravy!*

The Dots, who'd witnessed the entire scene, giggled.

I could feel how bright red I was, but I giggled, too. What else *could* I do? I just hoped to the heavens above that if I ever had a MOMENT WITH A BOY like that again, it wouldn't be until I was ready for it. Like, when I was sixty-eight or even eight-six. Because it was freaky being slack-jawed and marshmallow-brained like that! I had *no* desire to experience that sort of freakiness ever again.

Fortunately, Connor was just a normal boy, so I rejoined

him and put Mars Bar out of my head. I Gator-grabbed the bottom of Connor's T-shirt and shook him like a dog would shake a dog toy.

"Hey!" Connor cried. He tried to Gator-grab my shirt, and on his third attempt, he succeeded. Now we both had each other in a pincer grip. We circled each other, laughing.

Lily came up behind us and exclaimed, "Winnie! Connor! What in the world are you guys doing?"

"*I'm* not doing anything," I told Lily. I shuffled to the right and didn't let Connor go. "But as you see, there is a wild thing latched onto me."

"*Hey!*" Connor protested.

"But this *is* Wilderness Survival Camp, right?" I said, directing my words to Lily while keeping my eyes on Connor. "So you should be proud, because I'm doing exactly what you and Jake taught me to do!"

"And what would that be . . . ?" Lily said drily.

Did I really have to explain it to her? Apparently, I did.

"Well, as I said, there is wildness going on *right here in front of me*." I lunged forward. Connor tried to force me back, but he was so weak from laughing that I easily overpowered him.

"But you don't even have to worry," I huffed, "because look! I am fully and completely surviving!"

August

A ugust was Ty's birthday month, which was exciting, because birthdays were always exciting, as were the birthday parties that went with them. But Ty's parties were also exhausting, because of the littleness of everyone involved.

Ty's party this year was especially exhausting because of one mother who did something sneaky. The sneaky mother accidentally-on-purpose dropped off *not* just her four-year-old, Dylan, but also Dylan's seven-year-old brother, Chad.

"Is that all right?" the sneaky mom asked, wide-eyed. "So many parties allow siblings these days, so I just assumed . . ."

"Of course," Mom said, because of her good manners. "He's totally welcome to stay."

"Oh, thank God," the other mother said, her words pouring out in a relieved rush. She caught herself and pasted on a smile. "I mean—terrific!" She hastily exited the house. "I'll leave you to it, then. Bye, boys!"

Dylan was fine, but Chad, the seven-year-old, was a bad

egg. He jumped on the furniture and bounced off the walls and was so loud and hyper that he made my ears hurt.

When present-opening time came around, Chad grew even more annoying. Every time Ty unwrapped a new gift—*every single time*—Chad said, "I hope it's a dirty diaper. *Hahahaha*. I hope it's a dirty diaper."

I wanted to put a dirty diaper on Chad's head. I might have, if I wasn't ten and above such things.

When twelve o'clock rolled around and parents started showing up for their kids, Sandra tromped through the scraps of wrapping paper and plastic packaging and took my hand.

"Come on," she said. "We're going to the park, just the two of us. We deserve a sanity break."

"Yes, we do," I said, standing taller and feeling more in control than I had just two minutes earlier, when that Chad boy peered inside his goody bag and said, "SweeTARTS! I *hate* SweeTARTS!"

"Then don't eat them," I said, snatching the goody bag out of his hands. He wasn't even supposed to get a goody bag. He wasn't even one of the party guests!

He made an ugly face and tried to grab it back. I held it high above my head. Just then his mother arrived, and when she saw Chad jumping for his goody bag, she said, "Is there a problem?"

"Winnie," Mom said wearily.

So I scowled and gave Chad his goody bag, saying, "Here you go, little boy. I just thought maybe you didn't need any more sugar, since you're already so much taller than the other four-year-olds."

"Winnie," Mom said even more wearily. She shot an apologetic look at Chad's mother, which made me feel awful. Chad was seven, but *I* was ten. I was supposed to act mature regardless of how *im*mature other kids acted.

But at Memorial Park with Sandra, I was able to put my humiliation behind me. The day was lovely, there were no longer any little kids yelling and screaming and being sticky, and Sandra was treating me like someone she enjoyed spending time with.

Everything was perfect . . . except for one dang wasp that refused to leave us alone. First it dove for Sandra's Coke, making Sandra jerk her Coke away and cry, "Go a*way*, wasp! Go find your own Coke!"

The wasp barreled over to see if *I* had a Coke. I didn't, but it darted around my face and my hair anyway. Normally, I wasn't freaked out by bees or wasps or yellow jackets, and I thought it was silly when kids—and sometimes even grown-ups—screamed and started hyperventilating if a bee even looked at them from a thousand feet away.

This wasp, however, was a crazy lunatic wasp. It was the "Chad" of the wasp world, and after five or six minutes of its furious buzzing, Sandra groaned and said we might as well leave.

"What? No!" I protested. I wanted to keep having Sandra-time.

Sandra got to her feet. "Listen, that wasp isn't going to quit bugging us. August is when wasps get the crankiest, you know."

"Why?"

"Because they're in their final days. Because they know they're going to die as soon as fall comes."

"Well, that's silly. If I knew *I* was going to die, I would be nicer to everyone, not meaner."

"Maybe," she said. "Come on, let's get out of here."

I grabbed her leg. "Let's not—*please*? I don't want to go home."

"Who said anything about going home?" Sandra said. "Let's walk to Baskin-Robbins. We can get ice cream and eat it *inside,* away from these stupid wasps."

Oh, I thought, because that changed everything. Ice cream was delicious. Ice cream was the opposite of returning home and no longer having Sandra-time.

"Do the wasps really know they're in their final days?" I asked as I got to my feet. The Chad-wasp was still dive-bombing my head, and I felt the teeniest bit sorry for it.

"Yup, so do yourself a favor. For the next couple of weeks, stay out of their way."

A few days later, I passed Sandra's good advice along to Amanda, who nodded and said she already knew. In fact, the Wilsons had such a big wasp problem that Amanda's dad hung up a wasp catcher in their backyard. I'd never seen a wasp catcher before. It was a clear plastic tube the size of a cardboard toilet paper roll, but unlike a toilet paper roll, the wasp catcher had a bottom and a top. The top was yellow and triangular, like a roof, which was kind of cute—or so I thought at first.

Up close, however, I saw that the cute little wasp "house" was a HOUSE OF DEATH, because the tube was full to the brim with dead and dying wasps.

"Ew," I said. "Why do they go in there? Can't they see that it's a bad idea?"

Amanda shrugged. "Something inside smells yummy to them," she explained. "They push their way in, and then they can't get back out."

We studied the heap of wasp bodies. Fluff and dryness and broken wings. Tiny black leg-things. At the top of the tube, a still-alive wasp rammed repeatedly against the clear plastic.

"Okay, I'm officially grossed out," I announced, heading for the play structure her dad had built. It was awesome, with two swings, a climby rope, a slide, and a fort at the top with a rainbow awning. Sometimes we had tea parties on the flat wooden floor of the fort, and I loved the feeling of being alone with my best friend, tucked away from the rest of the world.

But today I wanted to fly. I got on one swing, and Amanda got on the other.

"Are you excited for school to start?" she asked. Her tan legs straightened and bent as she got herself going. She was wearing a lime green shirt with slices of watermelon all over it, and her shorts were the exact red of the watermelon slices. So was her hair bow. Amanda was very good at matching.

"Yup," I said. "I mean, I'll miss summer . . . but totally! You?"

"I've already picked out my first-day outfit," she said seriously. She pulled against the chains as she moved forward through the air. She slackened her grip and swung back. "Let me guess—you haven't."

"You got that right, sister," I said. First-day outfits didn't require planning. You just . . . put on some clothes, and ta-da! Instant outfit!

"But even with my outfit all picked out . . ." She sighed. "Oh, I don't know."

I felt a stab of shock. "Omigosh, Amanda. Are you *not* excited?"

"No, I am. I *am*. It's just . . ."

It's just what? I wanted to say. But I held back, because Mom said I needed to give people time to say things. She said sometimes the best thing a friend could do was listen.

Amanda sideways-looked at me. "If I tell you, will you swear not to laugh?"

"Of course. Spill."

"Well, it's just . . . it's just . . ."

I *kept* waiting. It was getting harder and harder, as it totally went against my natural instincts.

"Never mind. It's nothing." She made her lips form a smile shape, which anyone other than me might have fallen for. But her forehead was way scrunchier than usual, and plus, I was her BFF.

"Baloney," I said. "Stop scrunch-smiling and tell me what's bothering you, you silly custard!"

Her scrunch-smile turned into a sheepish *oops, ya-got-me* smile. But even though it was sheeplike, at least it was *real*.

"Oh, all right. I *am* excited for school to start. But . . . I'm scared, too." She lifted her eyebrows, Amanda language for, *Do you still like me?*

Of course I still like you! my stern downward-pointing eyebrows told her. I *was* baffled, however.

"Scared?" I said. "Of what?"

She made puppy-dog eyes and shrugged.

"Amanda, we're talking about *school* here. Trinity! Friends! The joyful laughter of happy, innocent children!"

"I know," she said meekly.

I frowned, because I could tell I hadn't eased her fears. How could I when I didn't know what they were? I racked my brain for things she was scared of just in general.

"There are no sharks at Trinity," I said, ticking *sharks* off with one finger. "There *might* be spiders, but if you see one, just tell me and I'll take care of it."

She nodded, and I made a mental note to pack a paper Dixie cup in my backpack, as Dixie cups were the perfect size for bamming down on top of spiders. Not to kill them! Just to trap them so that they could be relocated.

Amanda knew how much I loved rescuing spiders, so if spiders were the problem, my promise should have reassured her. But her expression remained troubled.

I blew out air from between my lips, making a *phbbbb* sound. "Well, there are no flesh-eating viruses making their way from elementary school to elementary school," I said. "At least, not that I'm aware of."

"I know."

"T. rexes died off a long time ago, in case you forgot, and killer ants are only in Africa." I wasn't completely sure of that, but close enough. "*Hmm.* Spontaneous combustion? Hurricanes? Harpoons?"

"Harpoons?" Amanda said. "Do you maybe mean *ty*phoons?"

Ah. Yes, I *did* mean typhoons, but I did some quick thinking to cover my mistake.

"What are you saying?" I said. "You're scared of a giant windstorm, but the thought of being stabbed by a long spear doesn't bother you one bit?"

She looked at me like I was a loon. It was a look I got a lot, and my usual response was to play it up by acting even loonier. Why not? I liked being a loon.

So I pumped vigorously, laughing like a maniac. "Ha ha HA! Ha ha! Ha ha ha ha ha!"

Amanda gazed at me. Not meanly, or in a *bad* way, but not in a particularly amused way, either.

I stopped with the maniacal laughter. I stopped pumping in such a fling-about way, too.

"Fine," I said. "If not typhoons, if not *harpoons*, what *are* you scared of? Won't you please just tell me?!"

She shifted her focus to the far end of the yard, where honeysuckle vines twined their way up a wooden trellis. "Just . . . fifth grade is different from fourth."

"And?"

"And that means things are going to be . . . *different*."

"And???"

"I don't know! What if I mess up?"

"Mess *what* up? You get straight As. You've gotten the perfect attendance award every year since first grade. What could you possibly mess up?"

She shrugged that shrug again, the shrug that made me feel powerless. In a tiny voice, she said, "Yeah, but what if I . . . *mmmfffle*?"

I squinted. Ty had said *mmmfffle* once. It was on the day we saw Hairy Speedo-Wearing Man at Garden Hills Pool, and *mmmfffle* was Ty's way of saying, *Winnie, help! I can see that man's privates!*

While I felt strongly that Amanda's *mmmfffle* meant

something else, I still heard it as a cry for help. I *wanted* to help . . . only I wasn't sure how. I'd already tried being goofy, and it hadn't done the trick.

But sometimes being a goof was all I could think to do, even when I secretly suspected it might not be the solution. I held onto the swing with one hand, cupped my ear with my other hand, and bellowed, "I can't hear you, little girl! Speak up!"

Amanda's cheeks turned pink. "Forget it. Seriously, just forget it."

"No, I refuse to forget it. And so what if fifth grade is different from fourth? It's supposed to be!"

"See? I knew you wouldn't understand."

"Wouldn't understand what? If things were always the same, they'd be boring. I understand that. I also think that *being different* is good, and I thought you did, too. Do you not?"

"No, I do. Mainly." She hesitated. "But it's easy for you, Winnie. You're not afraid of anything."

"Are you off your gourd?" I cried. "I'm afraid of *tons* of things, you silly custard!"

It was the second time I'd used that term, which I'd just made up today. *Silly custard. Silly, silly custard.* But when Amanda sighed, the back of my neck tingled, and I wondered if *I* was the silly custard.

Sometimes I got the feeling that I was *too* silly, especially when other people wanted to be serious. It was dawning on me that this was one of those times.

"I *am* scared of things," I said. "I'm not just saying that."

Her expression was cautious. "Like what?"

Well, here it was: the moment of truth. *Yes, Winnie,* a voice inside me taunted, knowing exactly what I was scared of and knowing exactly how embarrassing it would be to say it out loud. *Like what?*

I tried to think of the best way to explain, but my brain gears got stuck, and after several seconds, Amanda turned away. For once, she was the one not giving me enough time to find the right words.

"Wait!" I cried. I let the rest of the words tumble out despite their ridiculousness. "Flushing the toilet. I'm scared of flushing the toilet. All right?"

Amanda's head swiveled back toward me. We were still swinging, and we were almost—but not quite—in harmony. She searched my face as if she was trying to decide if I was putting her on.

"Not all toilets," I said. "Just the ones in my house. *You* know."

She gave me a small smile, because she did. I knew things about her that random people didn't, like how she twirled her hair when she was anxious, and she knew things about me in the exact same way, including the fact that the toilets in my old-as-the-hills house were louder than any other toilets in the world. She'd flushed them plenty of times herself, so she knew all about the tidal wave that rushed and swirled into the toilet bowl, roaring more ferociously than a sea lion.

According to Dad, it was because our plumbing system was installed before the invention of high-efficiency toilets.

According to me, they were white porcelain nightmares. Originally, it was just the roar of swirling water that scared me. But recently a new twist had been added to the mix. Her name was the Bathroom Lady, and I accidentally invented her, and she lived in the sewer. Her most burning desire was to reach up through the drains with her pruney, clawlike fingers and grab tasty children. And if she did? You were a goner.

As we swung, I told Amanda all about the Bathroom Lady. I told her every last detail, and Amanda giggled and wrinkled her nose, which made me giggle, too. I knew in my gut that there *was* no Bathroom Lady (probably), but nonetheless, it was a relief to share the burden of her.

"So, see?" I concluded. "Whatever it is you're afraid of, it's *not* going to sound stupid compared to what I just told you."

"Well . . . it might," Amanda said.

"I don't care. Tell me anyway."

She pushed her bottom lip out. The she pulled it in and pulled her top lip in as well, making her look like a prune.

Finally, she let her mouth go back to its normal position. "It's just that my mom said I should expect a lot of changes this year," she said. "Like that people are going to start making rules about who's friends with who, and girls are going to get more gossipy, and the whole issue of *boys*, and . . . yeah."

She tilted her head. "Does that make sense?"

No, because how could anyone make a rule about who was friends with who? As for "the whole issue of boys," well, what did that even mean? Frankly, being afraid of "the whole issue of boys" seemed as random as being afraid of the Bathroom Lady. Who was to say that either even existed?

But Amanda heard me out about my fears. She giggled, yes, but she didn't say, "Oh, you're so stupid. The Bathroom Lady—what a stupid thing to be scared of!"

I was determined to be just as supportive. "Okay, but how does your mom know all that stuff?" I asked. "Maybe that happened when she was ten, but that was *her* childhood. Not ours."

Amanda pulled her eyebrows together, maybe because I'd said the word *childhood*. "Childhood" wasn't a term kids generally used.

"I mean, are you afraid of boys? Because I'm not." I flashed briefly on that day in Wilderness Survival Day Camp, when I went to introduce myself to that cute boy named Mars Bar and turned into a frozen corn dog instead.

But that was a one-time occurrence. I banned it from my mind.

"And Amanda, *no one* can make rules about who we can be friends with," I said. "Anyway, aren't we pretty much friends with everybody?"

"I guess," Amanda said.

"You and Chantelle and I are *best* friends, but we're nice to everyone."

"True."

"As for gossip?" I did a nose-snortle to express my thoughts on that. I did it again, because it was fun. "Gossip is dumb."

She nodded. "Yeah. Okay."

I didn't know what else to say. Maybe there *wasn't* anything else to say. Maybe the best strategy was to *do* something instead.

"Dismount time!" I exclaimed. "I'm going to do the razzle-dazzle-fluff-'n'-puff. Ready?"

"On three," she said. "One, two—"

By the time I heard the three, I was already in the air, spazzing out and flailing my limbs before collapsing on the grass. Flushed, I scooched on my bottom toward the vines of honeysuckle at the edge of the yard. Stuck into the ground was a bee-yoo-tee-ful stepping-stone that Amanda made from a kit, with pretty stones embedded around her handprint. I plonked my booty on that bee-yoo-tee-ful thing and said, "What's my score?"

"Ten out of ten," Amanda said. "A razzly-dazzly delight."

"Why, thank you. And now, your turn."

Amanda pretended to consider her options, but we both knew she'd choose statue, because she always chose statue. She would sail from the swing and land solidly on her feet, which she called *sticking it*. She'd lift her arms triumphantly, and I'd award her an eleven out of ten.

"I'm waiting," I prompted in a singsong voice. A pesky wasp said *bzzzzz* into my ear, and I shook my head. Luckily, I'd put my hair up in doggy ears, and doggy ears were like cow tails: excellent at pesky-buzzing-insect shooing.

"Statue," she announced.

"Are you *sure*?" I said. "Are you *positive*? Why not try a triple flip this time? Or, I know! You could land in a handstand and then do a backbend to get to your feet."

"Statue," she said.

I smiled to myself, chalking that up as one more thing that would never change.

"Are you going to count, or not?"

"Right," I said. "One . . . two . . . three!"

Amanda soared through the summer air, her watermelon shirt a blur. Her blond hair streamed behind her, set off by the red of her red bow. She landed, stuck her chest out, and flung her hands high and wide.

"Wh-hoo!" I cheered. "Yes, ladies and germs, you saw it here first! The amazing Amanda Wilson performing her amazing—"

Amanda yelped. Her eyes bugged out, and she jumped around in a frenzy. "Help!" she cried. "Winnie! *Help!*"

I leaped up. "What is it? What's wrong?"

She slapped at her torso, panicked sobs and screeches making my pulse race.

"Is it a wasp?" I said. "Amanda—what *is* it?"

She couldn't get any words out, but whatever it was, it was *hurting* her, and it wasn't letting up.

"It's okay, you're okay," I said, my voice coming out stronger than I expected. I took hold of her watermelon shirt and tried to wrestle it off her, even as she grabbed the fabric and tried to pull it back down. "It's trapped in your shirt."

The shirt snagged on her fancy bow. I yanked, and finally the shirt was off. A wasp flew out, head-butted the honeysuckle trellis, and plummeted to the ground. A second later, it was up once again, zigzagging away.

"Omigosh," I said, panting. I took in Amanda's bare torso, which was dotted with three angry red welts. There might have been more, but I couldn't be sure since she'd wrapped her arms around herself to hide herself. "Thank goodness I was here, huh?"

She burst into a fresh round of sobs and fled toward her house. Like the wasp, her path was zigzaggy, because she refused to let go of her nakedness, and it threw her balance off.

"Go away!" she cried.

"Who? Me?"

"Yes, you, and it was a bumblebee, you stupid-head. Not a wasp. Now *go away*!"

My jaw dropped. *Stupid-head?* Amanda had never called me a stupid-head before. And it was so a wasp, and I *saved* her from it. Why was she acting like this?

Amanda's back door slammed shut, her house swallowing her up. I could follow, but she told me to go away.

Slowly, I walked toward the wooden fence that enclosed the backyard. With every step I took, I expected Amanda to reappear. I expected her to sniffle and apologize and say, "Come back. We'll make milk shakes."

I lifted the latch and slipped through the fence door.

Still no Amanda.

Bad thoughts came into my mind, and I couldn't make them go away. Sandra would say *pooey* to what I was thinking. She'd remind me that August was the cranky season for wasps, and though it was sad Amanda had been stung, it didn't *mean* anything.

But I was the one who knew the whole story. Amanda and I had been talking about scary things, and then something scary had happened—*right after we'd told each other that the things we were scared of wouldn't happen, because they weren't real.*

So what did that suggest about gossip and boys and fifth grade being different from fourth, different in a bad way?

And what about the Bathroom Lady? And two weeks from now, when school started, would there really be rules about friendship?

Sandra had warned me to stay away from wasps, and I'd warned Amanda. Even so, she'd gotten stung, and here I was walking home alone.

Did that mean it was impossible to stay away from the things that could hurt us? If so, what bad thing would happen next?

I shivered despite the heat of the day. I was afraid to find out.

Amanda and I made up before dinner. I picked up the phone to call her, and it was so weird, because she was already on the line! She'd decided to call me at practically the exact same time, but I picked up the phone before it even had a chance to ring!

We both said we were sorry, my words tumbling over hers and hers over mine. We promised we'd always be best friends and that nothing would ever change that, not the Bathroom Lady or boys or anything. And fifth grade would be great and not scary at all, we both decided. It would be great because we'd make it be great.

Amanda continued to insist it was a bumblebee that stung her, however.

"No, because bumblebees die after one sting, and you

were stung three separate times," I said. I wasn't just going to lie about it.

"Actually, four. One of the stings was near my . . ."

"Near your what?"

"Never mind," she said, and I knew it must have been on a naked part of her.

"See?" I said. "The proof is in the pudding."

"You don't know everything, Winnie. It was a bumblebee. They sting the worst, and I could feel its fuzziness."

I opened my mouth to argue. Then I changed my mind.

"Okay," I said, because maybe I *didn't* know everything. Maybe I didn't even need to know everything. As long as Amanda and I agreed on the important stuff, maybe I should just let the small stuff go.

September

Trinity's school year started on the Tuesday after Labor Day, and by Labor Day weekend, I was a fuzzy fuzzball bouncing off the walls. In a good way! There was just so much to be excited about, first and foremost being the fact that Amanda, Chantelle, and I were going to be in the same class this year!

There were two fifth grade teachers, Mrs. Tompkins and Ms. Meyers, and last week, they'd made their phone calls to the kids who were going to be in their classes. That's how it worked at Trinity. At the end of every summer, the teachers called whichever kids were on their lists and said, "I'm so pleased to have you in my classroom, *blah, blah, blah*." And this year, Ms. Meyers said *blah, blah, blah* to all three of us! It was a miracle!

I think the news made Amanda feel a *lot* less worried, since she now knew that I'd be right there beside her, as would Chantelle. At any rate, she never said another word about being scared. When she talked about school, she sounded happy, and that made me happy. 'Nuff said.

Another thing I was excited about was that Ty was starting preschool this year, so he'd be going to Trinity, too. Mom would sign him in every Monday, Wednesday, and Friday, and I couldn't help but grin at the thought of seeing him in the halls and waving at him and giving him high fives.

While Ty was just beginning his long long life of school, Sandra was at the opposite end of the stick. She'd gone to Trinity for elementary school, but for junior high she switched to a fancy prep school called Westminster. Westminster had an elementary school on its campus, too— and a high school—but Westminster's elementary school wasn't as warm and fuzzy as Trinity, and Mom and Dad wanted us to have "warm and fuzzy" for as long as we could.

At any rate, Westminster started on the same day as Trinity, which made for another exciting thing: As of Tuesday morning, Sandra would be a *freshman in high school*.

Whoa, that sounded old. Or, no. It didn't just sound old. Being in high school *was* old. I liked her being older than me, though, because of all the advice she gave me. Just last week she taught me a very helpful tip, which was that using a sweet *Mommy-oh-Mommy-please* voice really did work better than barking, "Hey! Lady! What's it take to get a Coke in this place?!"

Being a truck driver was fine, Sandra told me, and it was an excellent possible career choice. But for now I should be careful when it came to asking Mom to do things, because if Mom would launch into her I'm-not-your-servant,-you-know, speech, I'd either have to get my own Coke, or—more likely—be forbidden from having a Coke that day, period.

She also gave me the inside scoop about fifth grade. Lots of the things she told me were good, like how I was going to love science, because we'd get to dissect a real live earthworm. Only it would be dead. It would be a real live *dead* earthworm.

Some of the things she told me weren't as good, I admit it. Such as how it suddenly mattered what kind of notebooks you had, and how you weren't supposed to bring birthday cupcakes any more. But unlike the weird and vague warnings Mrs. Wilson had given Amanda, I trusted Sandra's advice, even the parts I didn't like.

Anyway, notebooks and cupcakes? *Pfff*, that's what I told myself about that. *No biggie.* I practiced what I preached, too, because on Sunday, Mom said, "Winnie, I'm going to the drugstore. Do you need new school notebooks?"

"Oh!" I said. "I totally do. Thanks."

"Cute ones, like the ones with the big-eyed monkeys you pointed out?"

For a teeny-tiny moment, I panicked. What if big-eyed monkey notebooks were *the wrong kind* of notebooks? I imagined me at the front of the class, clutching my wrong big-eyed notebook while the other kids laughed their heads off.

"Um . . . just boring ones," I said. I winced as I heard the words come out of my mouth.

"Boring ones? Are you sure? That doesn't sound like the Winnie I know."

It didn't sound like the Winnie I knew, either. "You're right, Mom. You are *so right*."

"So . . . big-eyed monkeys?" she said, amused.

"Yup, and the bigger-eyed the better." And it felt good. I wasn't going to worry about Sandra, I wasn't going to worry about Mrs. Wilson, and I certainly wasn't going to worry about something as goofy as notebooks. Goodness gravy.

Monday night, Ty asked if he could sleep in my room. I said sure, and Mom said sure, too.

"As long as you both go straight to sleep and don't stay up chatting," she couldn't help but add on. "You both have school tomorrow, you know."

"Omigosh, really?" I said. I clutched Ty. "Ty! We have school tomorrow! Did you have any idea, or did it totally creep up on you just like it creeped up on me?" I put my hand over my heart. "School! Tomorrow! *Aaaaaaaaagh!!!!!*" And I fell over dead on my bed, my arms and legs splayed wide.

"Okeydoke, Ty, I'm thinking tonight's not the best night to sleep in Winnie's room after all," Mom said. "I'm thinking someone's a little too wound up to have company tonight."

I bolted up. In a tender and concerned nurse voice, I said, "Ty? Are you too wound up to have company, Sweet Pea?"

"I was talking about you," Mom said, arching her eyebrows at me.

"I'm not wound up," I said.

"We'll be good. We pwomise," Ty said earnestly, and who could turn down a cutie-pie face like his?

Not Mom. She listened as we said our prayers, kissed us good night, told us she loved us, and turned off my bedroom light.

Once she was gone, Ty said, "Winnie?"

I rolled over onto my side. Even in the dark, I could make out his brown eyes gazing at me from behind his shock of hair. "Yeah?"

"Are there bullies at Twinity?"

"What?" I said. I was shocked. Really and truly shocked. "How do you even know what a bully is?"

"I don't know. Are there?"

I thought of television bullies, kids who stuffed other kids into lockers and made them eat yucky cheese. "Not at Trinity."

He let out a puff of relief.

"Hold on, though," I said. I loved Ty, and so I needed to be honest, just like Sandra was honest—usually—with me. "There aren't bullies. But there *might* be kids who . . . aren't exactly the most wonderful kids on the planet."

Under the covers, Ty pulled his knees toward his chest. "So what do I do? What do I do if I see one of those kids?"

"Well, I'll tell you."

He waited.

He waited some more.

"*When* will you tell me?" he asked.

"Right now," I said. It had taken me a minute to figure out my response, because I'd never had to deal with a bully myself. But then the answer came to me, and I knew it was right because I *felt* it to be right. "Remember that girl Erica, from the pool?"

"Is *she* going to be at my pweschool?"

"No. I'm just bringing her up as an example."

"How do you know she won't be at Twinity? Did you call her?"

"Erica is not going to show up randomly in your preschool class," I said firmly. "But even if she does—*which she won't*—maybe she's changed."

Ty furrowed his brow. I could tell he had little faith in a new and improved Erica.

"You're right. Erica probably *hasn't* changed, because kids like her take a long time to ripen."

"Like bananas?" Ty asked.

"Yes, and to tell the truth, she might not ever fully ripen, because that's the kind of person she is. But that's not the kind of person *you* are."

"Because I'm a *nice* banana."

"Exactly," I said. "And there won't be any mean kids at Trinity, but if there are, just walk away. If they say something mean, just walk away again, because guess what?"

"What?"

"Nobody gets to choose how to make you feel except you." I tapped Ty's nose. "Got it?"

"Okay."

"You're going to love school," I said. "School rocks."

"Okay." He squiggled up close, and the wrinkles in his forehead went away. "Love you, Winnie," he said, and just like that, he fell asleep.

The next morning, I walked into Ms. Meyers's class with butterflies in my stomach. The smell of whiteboard markers and new erasers filled the air, as well as the smell of fresh, clean hair. Everyone looked older. Karen's hair was short now, and Louise had pierced ears. I was jealous, and I told her so. Mom wouldn't let me get mine pierced until I was eleven!

I greeted person after person, swirling through squeals and fist-bumps and loud rowdy chatter. Energy bounced from one person to another, and it was so cool, because I could *feel* it. I felt that fifth grade energy, and I grabbed hold of it—or maybe it grabbed hold of me!—and I twirled out of pure joy.

When I came to a stop, I spotted Amanda. My face split into a grin, and I bellowed, "Amanda! Get over here, ya big lug!" I flung my arms wide. "Mama needs some lovin'!"

"Omigosh," Amanda said, pretending to be mortified. She came over, but she was too self-conscious to give me some lovin', so I picked her up around the waist.

"I've missed ya!" I said, still using my loud voice. It was fun to use my loud voice. "What'cha been up to, you old scoundrel?"

"Since last night when we talked on the phone, you mean?" She gave me a *you-are-weird* look, but she smiled despite herself.

Chantelle found us, and I dropped Amanda and hugged her.

"Chantelle! My favorite Chantelle in the world! How *are* you?"

"Squished," she said, wiggling away from me. She turned to Amanda. "Have you told her?"

"Told me what?" I said.

"I was waiting for you," Amanda said. "But you're here, so now I will!"

I looked at her suspiciously, unable to get a vibe on where this was going. Amanda seemed awfully perky, even perkier than normal. Possibly even *fake* perky, as if she was using all that perkiness to cover up something else.

"Here's the thing," she said, perching on my desk. She

was in her back-to-school outfit, which was a pink denim skirt and a white blouse with capped sleeves, and she looked adorable, of course. How could she not? She was Amanda. She was Amadorable! Amandable?

A mandible! Ha! We'd learned about mandibles last year in science. They were like jaws, like cricket jaws. I snapped my cricket jaws—*snap, snap, snap.*

"So what do you think?" Amanda said. She searched my face eagerly. "Do you?"

I stopped snapping. Had Amanda been talking the whole time I was mandible-ing? *Huh.* I did vaguely recall some background noise going on, but I'd accidentally tuned it out.

"Um . . . would you repeat the question?" I said.

Amanda and Chantelle shared a look, which I didn't like one bit. I only liked shared looks when they were shared with me.

"She was *saying* that we're in fifth grade now," Chantelle said.

"Yes!" I said, because I knew that. I *totally* knew that. I thrust my fist into the air. "Fifth grade! Yay, us!"

Chantelle grabbed my fist and quickly pulled it back down. *"Winnie,"* she said, almost if she were embarrassed.

"I was reminding you about how fifth grade is different from fourth grade," Amanda said. "You know. Like my mom said."

I narrowed my eyes. I thought Amanda had dropped all that dumb stuff her mom said. Since I myself had no desire to revisit the subject, I made spooky fingers to distract them. "*Oooooo*! Fifth grade! We might have to do"—I gulped audibly—"*decimals*!"

"We're being serious," Amanda said. "Could you be serious, too? Please?"

That made me feel weird. "Uh, o-kaaay."

"Chantelle and I talked it out, and . . . well . . . change doesn't have to be a *bad* thing, right? Being older means so many things, and some of them could be super-fun. And at first I was all worried, but Chantelle helped me not be."

I lifted my eyebrows incredulously. "*Chantelle* helped you not be worried?"

"And you did, too," Amanda hastened to add. "The point is . . . I mean, I guess we were maybe thinking . . ."

"Just say it," I said. I no longer even wanted to do spooky fingers, because when, exactly, did Amanda and Chantelle *do* all this thinking? And where was I? Why wasn't I doing all that thinking with them?

Again, Chantelle and Amanda looked at each other. It made something snap inside of me, and I clapped my hands in front of their faces. "Stop looking at each other! You've been doing a lot of thinking, and *what*?! What is this BIG THING you have to tell me?"

"Shhh!" Chantelle said.

"Thatit'stimewehadcrushesonboys," Amanda said in a rush.

I waited for the words to separate and make sense. They didn't. "Huh?"

"Boys," Chantelle said, boring her eyes into mine in what was supposed to be a meaningful way, I think.

It didn't seem meaningful to me. It seemed dumb, and also annoying, because it seemed obvious that Amanda had been talking to her mom again, and getting bizarre ideas planted into her brain.

"What about them?" I said in a steely tone.

Amanda and Chantelle *giggled*. They giggled, and Chantelle swept her arm to indicate the kids in our class.

"They're everywhere," she said, making Amanda giggle even harder.

"So?" I said. Yes, there were boys in our class. There were also desks. There was also a fish named Larry who lived in a bowl on Ms. Meyers's desk. Mr. Hutchinson, who taught sixth grade, even had a snake in his room. So what was the big fluffy deal about *boys*?

And yet that's all Amanda and Chantelle wanted to talk about, and not just Amanda and Chantelle, but Louise and Karen and Maxine, too.

Boys, boys, boys. Blah, blah, blah. And the worst part? The most ridiculous part in the history of the United States? Amanda and Chantelle thought we should each claim a boy to have a crush on. That was their top secret, stupid idea.

"I am not in that stage," I informed Amanda and Chantelle during lunch. Since it was warm out, we were eating on the playground.

They didn't believe me, so I informed them again. "I. Am. Not. In. That. Stage. Boys are fine. Sometimes. But does that mean we have to go boy crazy?"

"That's what girls do in fifth grade," Amanda said. She said it like it was a law, and not only that, but a law she approved of and found intoxicating. She *wanted* to be boy crazy, and so did the others. Everyone but me.

"We'll help you," Chantelle said.

"We will," Amanda said fervently. "We'll find the perfect crush for you."

I glanced at Amanda, and then at Chantelle. Notebooks I could handle. Cupcakes I could handle. But boys and boy craziness and crushes?

I was angry at Amanda's mom, a definite first. Because when Mrs. Wilson told Amanda all that malarkey about how she should expect a lot of changes this year, and how one of the changes would be the whole issue of *boys* . . . well, what was she thinking? Did she mean to send her darling daughter down this boy-crazy path? Was that her goal?

"I already know who my crush is," Chantelle said.

Amanda joined her in supplying the answer. "Tyrone!"

they said together, collapsing against each other in a girly, mushy pile of mashed potatoes.

I felt trapped. I also felt . . . itchy inside. Or something. If I walked away from their boy craziness, would someone else plop into their mashed-potato pile in my place?

Impossible—and yet deeply deeply dizzy-making.

Amanda took my peanut butter and jelly sandwich from me and placed it on my plastic bag. She took my hand, her eyes shining. "So . . . ? You're excited, right?"

I mustered what enthusiasm I could. My smile felt like it was made out of plaster. "Fifth grade boys, here we come!"

October

There was something rotten going on at Trinity. An evil force was at work, and I wasn't lying. Call it the moon, call it the ghost of Halloween past, call it *gargle-gurgle-glug*.

Or! *Or!* Speak the unspeakable and call the rottenness by its *real* name. Call it—gulp—gag—stagger about with hands at throat—*Alex Plotkin*.

Oh, that Alex. Just thinking about him made me narrow my eyes, because he was irritating and disgusting and deserved to be put in a cage. That's what Sandra said, and she didn't even know Alex. All she knew was that he was a boy, and in her opinion, *all* boys should be caged. For real, that's what she said.

It was after we'd gotten home from school. I'd gone in search of her, needing her advice, and I'd found her sitting on her bed doing her homework. I knocked lightly on her cracked-open door, but she didn't look up. I walked across the room and stood beside her. She still didn't look up.

I cleared my throat.

I cleared my throat again, with bonus sound effects suggesting the possibility of a hairball on the verge of being coughed up. Finally, *still* not lifting her head, she growled, "For heaven's sake. If you're going to say something, *say* it."

"Well, if you insist," I said.

I plopped down beside her, and she clutched her textbook to keep it from sliding off her lap. I wiggled and squirmed to settle myself into her mass of pillows—it took a while—and then I let it all pour out: Amanda's and Chantelle's boy craziness, the silliness of crushes, and the well-documented fact that I WAS NOT IN THAT STAGE YET.

I wasn't in that stage because I had far better ways to spend my time, I told Sandra. Like making sculptures out of wire coat hangers, bottle caps, shoe boxes, and Mom's jewelry stand, which was shaped like a tree. And which Mom reclaimed when she saw that I'd borrowed it, much to my annoyance.

That annoyance was an isty-bitsy spider compared to the gargantuan tarantula annoyance of Alex Plotkin, however. "Gargantuan" was one of my spelling words this week. It meant huge, enormous, and elephantine. So basically, Alex was as annoying as an elephant-sized tarantula, and I couldn't imagine *any*one not being annoyed (to say the least) if an elephant-sized tarantula showed up randomly on their doorstep and said, "Hey, how ya doin', you got any snacks?"

I explained all of this to Sandra, who said that if he was that bad, then I should put him in a cage and be done with it.

I lifted my eyebrows. I wasn't sure how practical her idea was, but I liked it. "Are you being serious?"

"As a heart attack," she replied, her eyes glued to her textbook. "Boys are nothing but trouble. If it were up to me, I'd lock them all up—and I'd keep them locked up until they were twenty-one or stopped making fart jokes, whichever came first."

I felt more hopeful than I had in weeks. If Sandra, who was in the ninth grade, would rather put a boy behind bars than have a crush on him, did that mean I wasn't a freak after all?

I bit the bottom left corner of my lip. It was new for me, this particular lip-biting expression. I'd invented it yesterday while staring at myself in the mirror, and it made me look pensive, I thought. Like a girl, but also a spy. A spy-girl, which I was considering dressing up as for Halloween. It wasn't written down in cement, though. A hobo was also up for grabs.

I released my lip, since I couldn't bite my lip *and* talk, and since Sandra hadn't noticed, anyway.

"So, this whole crush business," I said. "You're saying you don't have a crush on anyone? And that's allowed, even in high school?"

Sandra put down her pencil and regarded me for the first

time since I'd entered her room. Our faces were right next to each other, and her blue eyes seemed very . . . blue. My cheeks grew warm, but I held my ground. I needed to know.

"Well, first of all, *allowed* is the wrong word," she said. "There's not a rule book, you know. Not for fifth grade *or* high school."

"I know!" I said, because that was the same thing I'd told Amanda, back before fifth grade began. *There was no rule book.* Then it occurred to me that Sandra had avoided the real question. "So you *do* have a crush on someone?"

"Did I say that? No."

"Have you ever had a crush one someone?"

Her feet were crossed at the ankle, and she rotated the top one in a small circle. "Sure, but not this very second."

"Then when? How old were you? What grade were you in?"

She studied me. "Hmm. We're skipping that question. Now, back to Alex Plotkin."

"Bleh," I said.

"You seem to have strong feelings when it comes to this dude, Winnie. Which brings up an interesting question: Why?"

"Because he's gross!" I cried. "Because his mom said he wasn't allowed to pick his nose with his finger, so now he picks it with his big toe."

"Ew," Sandra said.

"Uh-huh. And once he ate dog food on a dare. He'll eat *anything* on a dare, and then he breathes on you."

"Double-ew!"

"Uh, yeah! And on the playground, he spins around and around with his eyes closed, and then he rams into people. He *claims* it's an accident, but it's not. He peeks, and that's how he picks his targets. The truth is he just likes to knock kids down."

Sandra looked like she'd smelled something bad, like chewed-up dog food mixed with boy-spit. "So . . . you *don't* have a crush on this Alex guy."

"What?!" I jumped off the bed, my skin crawling. "Ew ew *ew*! Sandra! *Ewwww!*"

She held up her hands. "I believe you. I just thought—"

"That *I* had a crush on *Alex*? No!"

"It's just that usually, when a girl talks and talks and talks about a boy, or vice versa, well, that's usually what it means."

I drew myself to my full height. "And again I say: I AM NOT IN THAT STAGE."

"Then what's the problem? Does he have a crush on you?"

"Yuck. No. *Gross*, Sandra."

I'd been a fool to talk about it, I realized, just as I'd been a fool to hope that Amanda's boy craziness would simply . . . fade away, like a ghostly spirit in the misty October air. It didn't. It just grew crazier, especially when the boys in our class learned that the girls were secretly auditioning them for possible crushdom.

"If he doesn't have a crush on you, who does he have a crush on?" Sandra asked.

I didn't say. As it turned out, I didn't have to.

"Amanda," Sandra filled in. "*Ahhhh.* And you're jealous."

"*No,*" I said. "I'm just grossed out, and I want him to go away." Maybe I wanted *everyone* to go away, everyone except Amanda.

Or, *omigosh.* Maybe I *was* jealous.

"Oh, Winnie," Sandra said.

Her sympathy made me feel sorry for myself.

"*All* the girls are picking boys to have crushes on," I said. "Everyone but me. And Amanda's so pretty, and she's got all those cute freckles, and since she hasn't picked someone yet, Alex thinks he has a chance, I guess."

Sandra put her arm around me. She tried to draw me toward her, but I was too wound up for a hug.

"But *I* think being boy crazy is d-u-m-b *dumb,*" I said. "We're in fifth grade! We have miles and miles to go before it's time to think about that stuff. I mean, Mom won't even let me get my *ears* pierced yet!"

"Winnie? Breathe. Unless you want to hyperventilate, you need to *breathe*, okay?"

I grew aware of my chest, which *was* rising and falling awfully quickly. And to tell the truth, I always had wanted to hyperventilate, kind of. Maybe this was my chance?

But, no. Sandra hugged me, and the solidness of her calmed me down despite myself. Not all the way, but enough that I didn't start seeing stars or anything.

"Being boy crazy *is* dumb, you're right," Sandra said. "But it'll pass, I promise."

"How do you know?"

"Because I'm me. I know everything."

I shot her a look.

"And because it's a fad," she said. "Fifth grade is a big year for fads. For me, it was Mexican jumping beans."

"Those toy ones with faces? That flip over in your palm, and then stand up straight?"

"Yep," Sandra said. "Dumb, huh?"

I remembered when Sandra built up her collection of Mexican jumping beans. I was in the first grade, and my class was studying koala bears. But Sandra didn't want to hear about koala bears. All she cared about were those beans, and she was always begging Mom to take her to Target to buy more.

"I thought you loved those little beans," I said.

Her cheeks turned slightly pink. "What can I say? Fads."

"Can I have them? If you don't want them anymore?"

"No," she said. "Back to Alex."

I groaned.

"If he's as disgusting as you say—"

"He *is*."

"Then why would Amanda like him?"

"She wouldn't. She *doesn't*."

"So there you go," Sandra said, relaxing against her bed's headboard. "You have nothing to worry about."

She was right. Alex was Alex, after all. He couldn't weasel in between me and Amanda no matter how hard he tried, and I *knew* that. There was nothing in the world for me to feel jealous about. Goodness gravy.

But seriously? A cage still would have been better.

There were sixteen kids in our class: eight boys and eight girls. Of the eight boys, two had already been plucked and chosen. Chantelle called dibs on Tyrone the day the craziness began, and Maxine claimed Mark soon after. She said it was because she liked his smile, but I think it was because "M and M" sounded good together.

With Tyrone and Mark out of the running, that left six boys up for grabs. *I* was not going to grab anyone, even if Amanda and Chantelle tortured me by making me lie on a bed of nails. Anyway, too bad for them if they did try that, because it wouldn't work. I'd seen a Discovery Channel special about lying on beds of nails, and I'd learned that the trick for surviving was to get on super-duper carefully and distribute your weight evenly.

There was a science museum in Arizona where you could actually could lie on a bed of nails—on the Discovery Channel show, they went there—and forever after, you'd have bragging rights. As in, *Oh, yes, these mosquitoes are quite a bother, aren't they?* + insert delicate yawn + *But I must say, they're* nothing *compared to that time I'd lain on a bed of nails.*

Amanda and Chantelle had *reluctantly* come to terms with my refusal to pick a crush, and in return, I'd *reluctantly* accepted the role of rah-rah girl. What that meant was that I squealed and did fast, soft claps with the rest of the girls when we got together on the playground and gossiped about who a particular girl *might* pick, and why, and how cute or *un*cute he was, and how his overall look might (or might not) be improved if he grew one of those walrus-style mustaches with long, curled-up ends.

Fine. No one was interested in the walrus mustache question but me. I was just trying to liven things up, because it was all so boring. The only part of the Crush Fad that wasn't boring was the part where Alex Plotkin called Amanda "milady" and opened doors for her and gave her stupid presents, like a heart made out of fuse beads.

But giving her a heart made out of fuse beads wasn't going to make her fall in love with him, and after art class, I told him so.

"Yeah, only it's not up to you, is it?"

"And you're not supposed to use the fuse beads for personal projects, and you're not allowed to use the iron unless Miss Huber's there to supervise. You totally know that, too."

"Miss Huber was sick," he said. He stepped within inches of me. "If the *sub*stitute didn't want me using the iron, then the *sub*stitute should have told me."

I waved my hand in front of my nose. He was exaggerating the *sub* at the beginning of substitute on purpose so that I'd have to smell his breath, BECAUSE HE'D ALMOST EATEN A **COCKROACH** DURING "MATH WITH PAT." Pat was a retired rocket scientist who volunteered at Trinity to make math fun, but today Pat forgot to show up.

Guess who—or what—did show up?

A cockroach. Yes, over by the quiet reading corner, and Maxine screamed, and Mark stomped on it with his big puffy tennis shoe, and Maxine swooned and said, "My hero."

Alex didn't like the idea of Mark being a hero, it seemed, because he said, "You stepped on a roach. Big whoop. I dare you to *eat* it."

Mark laughed in disbelief. "No way, dude. *You* eat it."

Alex held out his hand. "Fine. Give it to me."

"It's *squished*," Maxine said faintly. She lifted her eyes from the poor squished cockroach (and for the record, this was the *one and only* time I ever felt sorry for a cockroach, or ever would) and turned to her hero, Mark. "Do you think you can peel it off the floor?"

Mark got down on one knee. Robert handed him an index

card, and Mark scraped the squished roach off the carpet. A fiber of yarn came up, too, dangling from the yellowy-green roach guts.

"He's not really going to eat it, is he?" Amanda said. Her expression was horrified, and yet she couldn't seem to look away.

"No," I said. I raised my voice. "Even Alex isn't dumb enough to eat a dead roach."

"*Brave* enough, you mean," Alex said. He approached Amanda and knelt before her. "I will if you want me to, Amanda. *Do* you?"

"No!" Chantelle said, wrinkling her nose.

"Yes!" Louise said. She elbowed Karen, who joined her. "Eat the roach! Eat the roach!"

I swiveled my head to the door of our classroom. Where was Pat? Where was *any* teacher?

"Do it, dude," Mark said, but I noticed that he took a step back from Alex as soon as he passed off the index card with the roach on it. Maxine darted even farther back and hid behind him, giggling.

Alex grinned. Pinning his gaze on Amanda, he said, "So . . . ? It's your call, milady."

"Don't," I said.

"Do!" Louise said, along with half the other kids in the class. Even Chantelle flip-flopped positions and said, "Yeah, make him eat it!"

"It could have an egg sac inside it," I said.

"A squished egg sac," Alex said.

"You don't know," I said stubbornly. "Maybe some of the eggs are squished, but not all. And if you eat it, guess what?"

"Roach babies in your stomach!" David crowed. "Awesome!"

I grabbed the bottom of my chair and jump-scooted toward Amanda until our bodies were touching. What I was going to say was private. I didn't want Alex eavesdropping.

"He is just trying to impress you," I whispered into her ear. "Do *not* let him. Do *not* say yes, Amanda."

Amanda's skin was flushed, and she gave off a hum of excited energy. Even though she didn't like Alex—and I knew she didn't like Alex, because how could she?—I think she *did* like all the attention.

"Don't be mad, 'kay?" she said without looking at me.

"Amanda!" I said.

Alex waggled his eyebrows.

Amanda took a breath, then let it out in a giddy whoosh. "Yes." She covered her face with her hands, then peeked through her fingers. "Yes!"

Locking eyes with Amanda, Alex raised the index card and gave a toast. "For you," he said.

He angled his head, unhinged his jaw, and tilted the index card. Girls squealed. Boys did, too. One boy's screech was so high it hurt my brain.

But the roach didn't slide into Alex's waiting mouth. It stayed put, its broken brown body glued to the card by a smear of shiny . . . inside stuff.

There were sighs of relief and murmurs of disappointment. There was *lots* of nervous laughter.

"Use your teeth," David said. "Scrape it off."

Alex shrugged, and it seemed as if he was going to. But we would never know, because right at that moment—both wonderfully and horribly—ex–rocket scientist Pat huffed into the classroom.

Wonderfully, because *ha*, Alex was foiled.

Horribly, because *un-ha*, Alex wasn't truly put to the test. *Maybe* he would have done it. *Maybe* he'd have scraped that dead roach off the index card and swallowed it down, guts and all. But maybe he *wouldn't* have, and everyone would have said, "Boo! Boo! Boo on you, you stupid Alex Plotkin!"

As it stood, he got to claim the title and glory of Roach Eater without having ingested a single roach antennae. Not an antennae, not a leg, not even a . . . wingy thing.

And yet he acted as if he had roach-breath anyway—hence the *sub-sub-sub*stitute when he got in my face after art class. Amanda hadn't filed out of the room yet, and I fervently hoped it was because she was busy breaking Alex's fuse bead heart to pieces.

"Alex, you are playing with fire," I told him.

"Am I, Winnie?" He stepped even closer. "*Am* I?"

I tried to remember Sandra's words of wisdom: The Crush Fad was just a fad. Amanda would never pick Alex to be her boyfriend, and she would never *ever* pick Alex over me. If she did? *I* would have to eat a dead roach to win her back, and I really hated roaches.

"Yes, Alex, you are," I said. *I* stepped closer, so close our noses almost touched. So close I could see his eyebrows, which were abnormally pale. "Yes, Alex. You are."

At afternoon snack break, Alex sauntered over to the bean-bag cluster where Amanda, Chantelle, Maxine, and I were sitting.

"Excuse me, but these seats are taken," I said.

"Did I ask you?" he said. He dropped down next to Amanda, WHO GIGGLED. He held out his pack of cheese crackers and said, "Anyone want one?"

I reached for one just so I could crumble it up and throw it at him. He snatched the pack back.

"Let me rephrase. Anyone *other* than Winnie?"

"Alex, that's mean," Amanda said.

"Thank you," I said to Amanda. I turned to Alex. "But Alex doesn't scare me."

He lunged forward. *"BOO!"* he shouted.

Chantelle screamed. Maxine dropped her juice box, but luckily it didn't spill.

"Did *that* scare you?" he asked, stepping back and smugly taking a seat on the rug.

"Not at all," I said, using amazing self-control to keep my heart from leaping out of my chest and flopping around on the floor.

I smiled. I told Maxine I liked her earrings, which was true. Then, lightning quick, I sprung wolflike from my bean-bag. I bared my teeth and growled at Alex, and *everyone* screamed, including Alex.

"Ha," I gloated, sitting back on my haunches.

"My pants," Maxine said, and I glanced down to see a purple stain blooming on the white denim.

"Oh, gosh. I'm so sorry, Maxine."

She got up and grabbed the bathroom pass.

"I didn't mean to make her spill her juice box," I told the others.

"We know," Amanda said.

"I would like to point out, however, that Alex—not to name names—isn't nearly as brave as he wants everyone to think."

"Wrong," Alex said. "One time I stepped on a rusty nail and had to get forty-two tetanus shots."

"How fascinating," I said. "One time *I* lay on a whole bed of nails and didn't have to get a single tetanus shot."

"You *did*?" Amanda said. "When?"

Alex smirked. "Liar. One time my parents went out for dinner, and the babysitter forgot to come, so I stayed by myself for two whole hours."

"Well, one time I went downstairs in the middle of the

night for a snack," I lobbed back. "Everyone else was fully asleep, and I didn't even realize it. I was the *only person awake* in the whole house."

No one looked impressed. Amanda looked confused, and ready to be impressed if only she understood why, but Alex just snorted.

"Come on, ladies," he said to Amanda and Chantelle. "Let's stop the charade, shall we?" He leaned back on his palms. "Who here ate the dead roach, huh?"

"Uh, no one," I pointed out.

"Details," he said. "Minor details."

I glanced at Chantelle and Amanda. From the looks of it, his nearly eaten dead roach packed a punch, and it frightened me.

"Okay, okay, well . . . I didn't eat a dead roach, because that's disgusting. And again, neither did you." I swallowed. "But one time I touched a dead mouse. Didn't I, Amanda?"

"She did," Amanda said. "It was extremely dead, and his name was Henry, and Winnie dug a grave for him and buried him."

"Yep," I said. "Beat that."

Alex smiled a bad smile. "I saw a dead dog on the highway once."

"Ohhh! That's so sad!" Chantelle said.

I thought so, too. Dead dogs were on a different level

from dead mice *or* dead roaches, and I struggled with how best to respond.

"I saw it up close," he said before I got the chance. "My dad stopped the car and got out, because he wanted to make sure it was all the way dead."

"That's sick," I said.

"Shows how much you know, because if it wasn't all the way dead, he was going to put it out of its misery."

"How?" Amanda said. For the second time today, her blue eyes were fixed on Alex's smarmy face.

Amanda, snap out of it! I wanted to say. *Bad Alex! No! Yuck!*

"But it was all the way dead," Alex said. "Its skull was dented in."

Amanda put down her miniature quiche. Her mom always packed her good snacks. I had to pack my own snacks, so I usually ended up with a Thermos full of pepperoni slices. But even my pepperoni slices had lost their appeal, thanks to Alex.

"Oh, Alex!" Amanda said.

"And its eyeball had popped out," he said mournfully.

"Its *eyeball* popped out?" I said. "Really?"

Amanda shuddered. "If *I* saw a dead eyeball? *Ugh*. I don't even know what I'd do."

"I'd faint," Chantelle said.

"Me too," Amanda said.

"Not me," I said.

"Alex, you poor thing," Amanda said. "Seeing a dead dog—that's even worse than what we went through with Henry. Don't you think, Winnie?"

"For the dog," I muttered.

Alex gloated. He'd won that round, and he knew it. He once more held out his snack. "Cheese crackers, anyone?"

That night, I went to Mom. I told her the whole sordid story about how Alex was showing off for Amanda and how annoying it was.

"Hmmm," she said, chopping up carrots for a salad. "Don't you think you're a little young to be having crushes on boys?"

"I'm *not* having crushes. Amanda is. She just hasn't picked out who yet."

"She certainly doesn't need to be rushing into anything," Mom said. "There's plenty of time for boys later, like in college." She slid a row of carrot coins off the cutting board, grabbed a fresh carrot, and started hacking away. "Or *after* college. You do know how important college is, don't you?"

"Yes, Mother," I said. I squiggled in between her and the counter, forcing her to put down the knife. "But what do I *do*?"

"About what?"

"About Alex!"

"Oh," she said. "Well, Winnie, just ignore him. I know you hate it when I say that, but that's the best thing you can possibly do."

I made an exasperated sound. I *did* hate it when Mom, or any grown-up, said to ignore someone. *Oh, just ignore that boy in werewolf's clothing, little girl,* as if ignoring people was as easy as eating a delicious chocolate chip cookie.

"Mom, that is the most unhelpful advice ever," I said. "Try again."

"Sorry, sweetie, but it's the best I've got," she said. She attempted to lean past me to get at the carrot. When that didn't work, she set down the knife, placed her hands on my shoulders, and moved me out of her way.

"What you've got to remember—and this has always been hard for you, Winnie—is that you can't control how other people act. That means you can't control what Alex does or doesn't do. You can only control what *you* do."

"Thanks, Mom. Great. Yeah."

I controlled what I did by exiting the kitchen. I searched the house for Sandra, but found Ty instead. He was in the long hall just past the dining room, wrapped almost entirely in duct tape. Only his eyes and his nostrils were visible. His arms extended unnaturally from his body, and his legs were stiff, stubby tree trunks.

"Hi, Ty," I said. "Are you practicing for Halloween?"

He nodded emphatically and made some *oomphuhly* sounds.

"Are you a mummy?"

He staggered toward me. He was very realistic.

"Looking good," I said, patting him on his duct-taped head. I moved to pass him, but he hop-lurched to block me. He widened his eyes and made more *oomphuhly* sounds, and it struck me that they weren't happy *oomphs*. They were desperately unhappy *oomphs*. I'd just been too wrapped up in my own problems—"wrapped up," ha—to notice.

"Oh, Ty." I tilted my head, studying him. I went around him, grabbed his torso from beneath his armpits, and lugged him backward up the stairs. His feet bumped along behind.

"You're lucky I'm so strong," I panted.

I stopped for a break at the halfway point, but when I relaxed my hold on him, he started sliding away. This time his head made the bumping sounds, and his *oomphs* were more of the *owwie* sort, I'd say.

"Whoa!" I cried, chasing after him. "Get back here, you mummy!"

It took a full hour to unwrap the little guy, and I learned an interesting fact, which was that boys were wimpier than girls when it came to neck hair. Ty was, anyway. Maybe it was because girls put their hair in ponytails, and so we were accustomed to the sensation of tugging?

I wished I had a video camera so that I could record the whole long process, but since I didn't, I decided I'd become a movie director when I grew up and make a movie of how one determined ten-year-old managed to free her helpless little brother from yards and yards of duct tape.

There was squirming, there was whimpering, and there was a *tiny* bit of actual crying. The crying came from the unexpected discovery of a Dum Dum duct-taped to the base of Ty's skull, right where those sensitive neck hairs were. Apparently Ty thought a partially sucked butterscotch-flavored one would make an excellent zombie antenna. Apparently, he forgot that zombies didn't have antennas.

Ooo! Since my movie would involve zombies, maybe it could be a made-for-TV Halloween special! I'd cast Alex Plotkin as the ugliest, dum-dum-iest zombie leader, and the plot twist would be that Ty *wasn't* a zombie, despite all appearances. The plot twist would be that the dum-dum zombie leader tried to steal Ty away and *make* him a zombie, but the determined girl saved Ty and locked the mean dum-dum zombie in a cage for all of eternity. Sometimes she would throw in a chicken bone. Sometimes just pebbles.

To play the role of the determined ten-year-old, I'd pick a brown-eyed, brown-haired girl, although with longer hair then I really had, and with pierced ears. For Ty, I'd choose a boy with lung power, since he'd have to scream through layers and layers of duct tape. Also, he'd need to have lots of hair, since big hair ball-y clumps of it would end up being yanked out.

And *ooo, ooo!* I could make a hair ball toy to go into McDonald's Happy Meal bags! It could be called Hair ball-y, the lovable, huggable hair ball. Each hair ball could be made of real hair—maybe from a llama?—with glued-on googly eyes. The girl hair balls could have pink bows, and the boy hair balls could wear tiny ball caps.

The thought of those cute toy hair balls cheered me up so much that I gave up on finding Sandra and asking for advice concerning Amanda. Instead, as soon as Ty was duct tape–free, I plain and simply called Amanda herself.

"You're not considering *Alex* to have a crush on, are you?" I asked her flat out.

"What?!" she said. "No. *Ew.*"

"Are you sure?"

"Alex *Plotkin*? Winnie, I am *very* sure."

"Even with the dead eyeball?"

"*Especially* with the dead eyeball. *Ew.* Why would I have a crush on a boy who touched a dead eyeball?"

Technically, Alex hadn't *touched* the dead eyeball, not according to his story. But why nitpick?

"Well, good," I said.

"Did you really think I might?"

"Yes, and that you two would get married and forget all about me and never sit with me at lunch again."

"You're crazy," she said. "I will always sit with you at lunch, you silly custard."

Silly custard?! Did Amanda just call me a silly custard? She did! She just used the nickname *I* made up for *her*, and it made me so happy! Now we were silly custards together!!!

"And also, I might be over my crush phase for a while," she confessed.

"Really?"

"Really. Why rush it, right?"

"Uh, right," I said, wondering if all mothers gave their daughters the same speeches on the exact same days. Maybe they had calendars for that sort of thing? "Hey, wanna be spy-girls for Halloween?"

"No. I'm going as a princess. Do you want to be a princess with me?"

"No. Maybe. Except, *no*. Like you said, why rush it?"

"Okay, I'm confused. What do crushes and princesses have to do with each other?"

I giggled. "Um, they both like pineapples?"

"Winnie, you truly are weird," Amanda said.

"I know," I said happily.

Alex may have won the battle of the dangling eyeball, but I won Amanda.

No, strike that, because I'd never *lost* Amanda.

But I wanted to win something. Hmm, what did I win?

Ah-ha! I knew! I won the Happy-to-Be-Weird Award, and not for the first time. And I hadn't won by being a helpless princess or a piece of crushed pineapple, either. I'd won just by being me.

November

Thanksgiving was one of my favorite holidays in the world, right up there with Christmas, Halloween, Valentine's Day, and National "I Hate Olives" Day.

Today in school we were doing our annual Thanksgiving-based activity. Every year we did Thanksgiving activities, but every year it was something different. In third grade, we made turkeys out of our handprints, which was preschool-ish, but still fun. In fourth grade, we made homemade applesauce, just like the Pilgrims did. We made it for a big Thanksgiving feast for the whole school.

This year, we'd be churning butter for the feast, but not today. Today we were making acrostics. Ms. Meyers had us write the word *Thanksgiving* on a piece of paper, with the letters going down the page instead of across. Now we were coming up with things we were thankful for that began with each of twelve letters. They could be single words or whole sentences, whatever we wanted as long as what we wrote was appropriate, Ms. Meyers said. She looked hard at Alex Plotkin when she said that, and when she turned away, I smiled evilly and mouthed, "Yeah, *Alex*."

T was easy. I picked a green pen and neatly wrote "urtles," because turtles were awesome. If I didn't grow up to be a movie director, I'd probably be a marine biologist and study sea turtles, because sea turtles could live to be over a hundred years old, and how cool was that? And on weekends, I could work at Sea World and train the dolphins.

Sea World! Yes! I skipped ahead and wrote that down for the *S* of Thanksgiving. I had never been to Sea World, but I wanted to, and Ms. Meyers told us that writing things down was an excellent way of "setting your intentions." She said that when we wrote down a goal or a dream or whatever, it helped to firm it up in your brain so that it would be more likely to actually happen.

If she was telling the truth, then I should use one of my valuable letters to set my intentions regarding Alex. (But only one, because he didn't deserve more than that.)

Hrmm. *H* wasn't a good one, because *H* made me think of hate, and I didn't *hate* Alex. Plus you couldn't be thankful for hating someone, because that would just be weird. And sad. So *H* was out of the running as far as Alex went. For *H,* I decided to go with "aving fun with friends." I drew a smiley face to go along with it.

A was next. Oh! Perfect! As the *A* itself was already there, I bent over my desk and added, "lex Plotkin not living in my basement." Was I thankful for that? WAS I EVER!

Did I want to firm up the reality of that never happening? DID I EVER!

I struggled for a few minutes with *N*. *N* was a tough nut to crack. Then I giggled, because *der*.

"uts," I penned in after the *N*. "Especially the ones in peanut M&M's."

I wrote and wrote. This was fun. Soon my acrostic was almost done, and it looked this this:

Things I Am Thankful For

Turtles

Having fun with friends

Alex Plotkin not living in my basement

Nuts, especially the ones in peanut M&M's

Krispy Kreme doughnuts!

Sea World

Getting to go to the Staute of Liberty

Imagination (mine)

Very best family EVER!!!!!!

Interesting and highly informative shows on the Discovery Channel

Not having to eat giblets, and also not being a giblet

G

I pooched out my lips. I was *almost* done. Lots of kids were only halfway done, or not even that close, but all I had left was that second *G*. What to put for that second *G*???

The answer was handed to me out of thin air, because

just then, Ms. Meyers said, "Okay, kids, finish up. We've got ten minutes before the bus gets here."

And my brain went *wheee!* Because *of course*—how could I have forgotten? The bus Ms. Meyers was talking about was coming to take all of us kids—both fifth grade classes—on a field trip! *A field trip to the World of Coca-Cola*, because Karen's mom worked for Coke, and she got special permission for us to go.

I laughed and slapped my desk when Ms. Meyers told us about it. When I showed Sandra the permission slip, I laughed some more. I didn't have my desk to slap, so I slapped Sandra's back.

"Ouch," Sandra said, lunging forward dramatically and *pretending* my slap had hurt.

"But look!" I said, pointing out the World of Coca-Cola part on the permission slip.

She closed her eyes, pressing her fingertips to her forehead. "Oh, good Lord."

"Yep!" I crowed. "The day has come: I'm going to get to be a tourist in my very own city! So *who* goes to the World of Coke? I do! I do!"

Now, twining my feet around the legs of my desk, I grinned at that lonely *G* and filled in "oing to the World of Coke! *Yahoo-eee-hoo-eee-hoo-eeeeeee!*"

"Winnie?" Ms. Meyers said, standing above me. I jumped, and my knee bonked the underside of my desk, knocking my pencil and paper to the floor.

"Smooth," Alex said, but his voice sounded oddly far away. I lifted my head and saw that he was all the way across the room, lined up at the door with the rest of the class. When in the world had that happened?

"Just leave her," Alex suggested.

"Oh, pooey on you," I shot back.

"Pooey on you both," Ms. Meyers said, which shocked me, and then made me grin. Secretly, and without letting Alex see, she smiled a small smile just for me. "Come on, Winnie. It's time to go."

The World of Coca-Cola was, in a word, *Coketastic*. We entered through the lobby, which was filled with statues of Coke bottles taller than me. The walls were decorated with photos of happy, smiling people, and though they weren't drinking Coke in the pictures, I was pretty sure we supposed to think they had Cokes in their hands and their hands just happened to be out of sight, or that they had just finished swigging a delicious Coke, or that they were about to swig a delicious Coke and that's why they were so happy.

In addition to the photos and the statues, the lobby was also filled with REAL LIVE TOURISTS. I whispered to Amanda and Chantelle that we should be extra friendly and polite, so that we'd make a good impression.

"How do you know they're tourists?" Chantelle asked after I complimented an old man on his walking cane.

"Because of their shirts," I said, doing an arm sweep to

draw their attention to the vast display. Some shirts had the Coke logo, some were Braves baseball jerseys, and one lady had on a lime green T-shirt that said *Hotlanta* in pink letters.

"Wow," Chantelle said.

"Omigosh, I have never seen so many Atlanta shirts in my life," Amanda said.

"Yup," I said. My point exactly.

One boy—he was maybe seven or eight—had on a shirt that made me grouchy, however. His shirt said, *I'm kind of a BIG DEAL in ATLANTA,* but guess what? He wasn't. He wasn't a big deal at all, because if he was, then I would know him, or at least know *of* him, and I didn't.

He was clearly a tourist, I concluded, and that just added to his irksomeness. Because if he was a tourist, that meant he lived somewhere else. If he lived somewhere else, that meant that he was an outsider when it came to Atlanta, just like I'd been an outsider in New York. And in New York, had I gone around bragging that I was a big deal?

No. In fact, I'd done the opposite. I'd behaved just like Aunt Lucy told me to, in order to fit in with the real New Yorkers.

Whoa. If there were rules for New Yorkers—like don't be spazzy if you see a famous person, fold your pizza before eating it, know how to hail a taxi with confidence—were there rules for people who lived in Atlanta? If so, did I follow them?

This was confusing, because I pretty much only approved of rules when it came to board games and red lights. Like Sandra, I didn't believe in rules for how to be a fifth grader or how to be a ninth grader, and as I'd taught Ty, I didn't believe there were rules for how to be a boy versus how to be a girl.

But I *did* like Coke. That was an unofficial Atlanta rule. And I *loved* Krispy Kreme doughnuts, although like most people in Atlanta, I'd only eat them when they were fresh off the doughnut conveyor belt. A cold Krispy Kreme doughnut wasn't a real Krispy Kreme doughnut. A Krispy Kreme doughnut sold at the grocery store as a fund-raiser definitely wasn't a real Krispy Kreme doughtnut.

On the other hand, I preferred to be barefoot than to wear fancy shoes. I hate purses and other "proper Southern lady" things like lipstick (*blech!*) and pantyhose (*double blech!*).

Maybe what it boiled down to was this: I was proud to be an Atlanta girl, but I had no desire to be just like every *other* girl in Atlanta. I didn't want to fit inside a cookie cutter—or rather a Coke bottle! *Ha!* I just wanted to be me. And since I *was* me, and since I was doing a pretty good job of it (in my opinion), then who should be wearing the *I'm kind of a BIG DEAL in ATLANTA* shirt?

That's right: ME, a true Atlanta insider, who nonetheless wasn't afraid to be an outsider when the mood struck.

I got so wrapped up in my insider-outsider thoughts—and

with wanting that boy's shirt—that I almost got left behind when the other fifth graders exited the lobby. Amanda had to grab my elbow and say, "Winnie, snap out of it. It's time to go in search of the secret formula!"

"Huh?"

She dragged me up the stairs to the second level, where the whole grade was filing into a theater. A sign at the door said, "Embark on a quest to uncover the mysterious secret formula for Coca-Cola! But beware: You're in for a bumpy ride!"

Chantelle and Maxine were ahead of us, accepting 3-D glasses from a man with wild hair who was dressed in a white lab coat. We fell in behind them and got our own pairs. They had the Coke logo on them. I immediately put mine on.

"I am a *ma-a-a-ad* scientist!" I said in a mad scientist voice. I waved my hands around madly. "I will find the secret formula or die trying!"

A girl named Mindy looked at me not as if I was a mad scientist, but as if I was a nutcase who deserved to be locked up. I didn't know Mindy very well, because she was new to Trinity this year, and plus she was in the other fifth grade class. Still, I dropped my mad scientist act and grinned at her. She didn't grin back.

The theater went dark once everyone was inside, and the movie started. It was about this weird guy named Professor

Rigsby who was trying to figure out why Coke was so good, and maybe it was kind of dumb, but I loved it anyway. There was a ferret that leaped out at us, and floating fruits, and when Professor Rigsby went to visit the Coke factory, he traveled there in a giant rumbling Coke can. And when the can on the screen rumbled, our seats rumbled!

I was *not* expecting that, and I squealed and grabbed my armrests. Amanda squealed and grabbed me. Our seats moved other times, too, lurching us forward and shaking us up and tilting us from side to side. I guess that's what the sign meant by telling us we were in for a bumpy ride.

At one point, Professor Rigsby took us to see the water filtration system, and *real water* misted up from under our seats. We squealed again. I leaned over to see if there were hoses down there, but it was too dark for me to see. We got misted again when the movie showed a giant water fountain, but that time we were more prepared. We also got wind blown in our faces and jostled a lot more. It was awesome.

After the movie, we were allowed to wander around on our own. Amanda, Chantelle, and I stuck together, and we learned lots of freaky facts about Coke. Like, in Japan, they sell *soup* in Coke cans, and that when Coke first came out, it cost five cents a glass.

"Oh, oh!" I said, spotting the part of the museum I'd been looking for since we got there. "The tasting room! Come on!"

We rushed inside and saw most of our class already in there. The whole room was one big soda fountain, pretty much, only instead of six drinks to choose from, we had *sixty*. Sixty different soft drinks, from all over the world! Sugar sugar sugar! And *caffeine*!

"Oh my God," I overheard Ms. Meyers say to Mrs. Tompkins after Alex Plotkin burped so loudly that a security guard had to tell him to quiet down. "*Whose* idea was this?"

My favorite drink was Spar-berry, from Zimbabwe. It was like sparkling berries of delight. My least favorite was from Italy. It was called Beverly, and it was . . . it was . . . *blegh*. It was awful, and why anyone would drink it on purpose was a mystery I doubted anyone could figure out, even Professor Rigsby.

We ended our tour by filing in with a big group of tourists to view a second movie. This one was peaceful and relaxing, and the seats didn't move. Basically it was one big commercial made up of all the squillions of Coke commercials that had ever existed. I liked it, especially one commercial about an adorable baby polar bear, and another commercial where tons of people got together and sang, "I'd Like to Buy the World a Coke."

It made me realize that really, the entire World of Coke was one big commercial. But I didn't care. I loved the World of Coke. I loved everything about it.

And then:

Something *moved* on my armrest, and I jumped and cried out.

"What?" Amanda said. "Did your seat move?"

"Not fair!" Chantelle said. "Mine didn't!"

"Girls. *Shhhh,*" Ms. Meyers said, giving us a stern look from way down at the end of the aisle.

I zipped my lips and did some dramatic pointing. I unzipped them just enough to whisper, "My seat did not move. My seat has a *toe* on it!"

I was sitting in between Amanda and Chantelle, and they both leaned in to check my armrest. Propped up on it was *a real live human toe*, probably female because of the chipped red polish, and in desperate need of lotion.

"Ew!" Amanda whispered.

"I know!" I bent over and looked beneath my seat, where I spotted two *empty* sandals. In Atlanta, you could wear sandals in November, because it rarely got cold. I sat back up straight. Jerking my thumb over my shoulder, I whispered, "It belongs to the lady behind me."

"You think?" Chantelle said.

"Well, it better!" I huffed. If it didn't, *omigosh.* I imagined the headline: Disembodied Toe Floats through World of Coke, Terrorizing Small Children! *Ahhhhhh!*

"Make her move it," I told Chantelle.

"Excuse me? *You* make her move it," Chantelle said.

"Why me?"

"Because it's *your* toe!"

"It is not *my* toe, and I am *terribly* offended!" I folded my arms over my chest. "The only way to make it up to me is if you move it."

She rolled her eyes.

"Fine," I grumbled. I turned to Amanda, resting my head on her shoulder and batting my eyelashes. "Amanda? Will you move it?" Pwease?"

"No way," Amanda said. She giggled. "Just . . . poke it."

"Or tell the lady to move it," Chantelle said. She peeked behind us, then dropped back with a plop. "Except never mind. I think she's asleep."

Asleep? When she was supposed to be appreciating Atlanta by watching Coke commercials?! What kind of horrible tourist was she?!

I looked at the toe. The toe looked back. It was one *ugly* toe. What if it had a fungus? Its bad-lady owner clearly didn't take good care of it. What if it had a flesh-eating toe fungus, and it spread to me, and when the Coke movie ended, all that would remain in my seat was a pile of skin flakes and a *telltale chip of red toenail polish*?

"A girl's got to do what a girl's got to do," I said under my breath.

So I leaned over, fished around in my backpack, and sat up with my hot pink Hello Kitty gel pen.

"No!" Amanda said, her eyes wide with horror, delight, or both.

"*Ready, Kitty?*" I whispered.

The Hello Kitty charm at the top of the pen bobbled her head. "Ready!" she said in a high-pitched kitty voice.

I gave that toe a quick, fast jab, and Chantelle and Amanda gasped. But the toe? The toe didn't move. The toe didn't even flinch!

I. Was. Shocked.

I poked it again. It didn't move *again*.

"Well, folks, I'm sorry it's come to this, but it has," I said.

"Winnie?" Amanda said nervously.

I couldn't let her distract me, so I pretended she was a moth.

"*Winnie,*" Chantelle said.

I turned her into a moth, too.

I twisted sideways, uncapped my gel pen, and drew two eyes on that toe. The toe didn't move, so I added a scowl, two angry eyebrows, and a pointy nose. Then freckles. Then zigzaggy electrified hair.

The toe moved. I quick sucked in my breath. I froze all my body parts except for my eyes, which searched for a place to hide my pen.

Amanda's lap! Yes! I placed the pen on her jeans, then folded my hands in my lap like a good little Coke girl.

"Winnie, no!" Amanda whisper-squealed, flicking it off her.

"*Girls,*" Ms. Meyers said, bending forward at the waist

and shooting us a sternier stern look than her first stern look.

"Sorry!" I mouthed. I pointed at Amanda, but above Amanda's head so Amanda couldn't see. I waggled my eyebrows to say, *She's a wild one, I know, but I'll calm her down.*

You better, Ms. Meyers said with a head tilt.

I gave her a thumb's-up, and then I settled back in my seat. I looked at the toe and smiled, imagining what its owner would think when she saw. If she saw, even. People didn't always examine the bottoms of their own toes.

If she did see, I hoped she'd be amazed. Amazed and *thankful,* because without even asking, she'd received a genuine autograph from a genuine girl from Atlanta. Not just any girl, but a girl who was, frankly, a pretty big deal. A girl who was me.

December

Eeeeee! I *loved* Christmas. I loved it and wanted to marry it, and I would never spell it that bad way with the "X" plus the "mas." One night about a week before school let out for Christmas break, I gave a stirring speech during dinner about that very subject. About how spelling it like that really did take *Christ* out of *Christmas*, only instead of applauding, dumb bunny Sandra jumped in and tried to show off how smart *she* was and how un-smart *I* was.

"What about people who don't believe in Christ?" she said. "What about Jewish people and Muslims and"—her eyes scrunched, then widened—"Rastafarians? Really, Winnie. Have you ever stopped to think about the Rastafarians?"

I pointed at her with a green bean. "First of all, I don't know what a Rastafarian is. And second of all, I'm not talking about them. I'm talking about me. I, Winnie Perry, refuse to take Christ out of Christmas, and the Rasta-whatever-ians can either like it or lump it. But for the record, I am more than happy to share Christmas with everyone."

"Great, but not everyone wants to share Christmas with

you," she said. "How do you think all the non-Christians feel when you go trotting around saying, 'La la la! I'm so special because I'm a *Christian*!'"

"I don't say that."

"You are right now."

I smiled triumphantly. "Ahhhh-*HA*! And that is where the cookie crumbles, because I'm not standing on the street with a foghorn, now am I?"

"Bullhorn," Dad said.

"Bullhorn," I said. "Nope, I'm simply having a lovely conversation with my family as we enjoy a lovely dinner." I turned to Mom. "And Mother? *Thank you* for this delicious meal."

"You're welcome," she said. "Thank you for saying thank you."

"Thank *you* for saying thank you for saying thank you."

"Oh good grief," Sandra said.

I turned back to her. "Anyway, God is God is God whether you're a Jewish person or a Muslim or a Rasta-whatever-ian. That's what I think, and so does Maxine, who *just happens* to be Jewish. And last week, her mom came in and taught us all about Judaism and made us potato latkes."

I called up the potato latkes' salty, crispy deliciousness and said, "*Mmmm.* Do you know how to make potato latkes, Mom?"

"Sorry," she said. "I can make a mean red velvet cake, though."

"Could you *learn* to make potato latkes?"

"I'll look into it," she said. "So Maxine's mom talked to your class about Judaism? That's great."

"She does that *every* year, Mom. Dreidel, gelt, menorahs . . ." I put down my green bean, because I didn't like green beans. Tearing off some bread for myself, I said, "I'm practically Jewish myself by now."

Sandra snorted.

I gave her a haughty look. "And for the record, Maxine and her family celebrate Christmas *and* Hanukkah. Unlike some people I know, they do want to share the joyful story of how baby Jesus came to be born."

Sandra gestured at my plate. "My, oh my. You certainly have a long way to go on your green beans, don't you?"

I stuck my tongue out at her. She stuck her tongue out at me.

"Girls," Dad said.

"How *was* baby Jesus born?" Ty asked, sticking a green bean up each nostril. He hated green beans even more than me.

Ooo, excellent question, I thought. Not to brag, but just as I was an expert on Judaism, I knew quite a lot about "the birds and the bees," as adults liked to put it. My specialty was conjoined twins. I'd seen a Discovery Channel show about two sisters whose heads were connected, and it was quite eye-opening.

Not that baby Jesus was a conjoined twin.

"Do you mean just Jesus, or how babies are made in general?" I asked.

"Both," Ty said.

Dad opened his mouth, then closed it. I opened *my* mouth, but Mom jumped in before I could say anything.

"Ok-a-a-ay," she said. "No more talking. Just eating. And all three of you better eat every single bean on your plates, or those beans are what you'll find waiting for you under the Christmas tree."

Ty started cramming beans into his mouth like a crazy person. His chipmunk cheeks went up and down as he chewed.

"Ty's eating his beans!" I exclaimed. "Beans, beans, the musical fruit. The more you eat, the more you—"

"Winnie," Dad warned. "Why don't you get to work on your own beans, *hmm*?"

"Fine, fine." I stabbed two beans with my fork and shoved them in my mouth. *Blech.*

Sandra's gaze traveled around the table as if she had no idea how she ended up in this family. But guess what? She *did* end up in this family. She was one of us, and without her, we wouldn't *be* us.

"I have just one thing to say," she announced.

"So say it," I said with my mouth full.

"Make that two things."

"And those two things would be . . . ?"

She munched off the tip-top of a single bean. She chewed, swallowed, and patted her mouth with her napkin.

"Goodness gravy, you slowpoke," I said. "Dad, would you poke that slowpoke?"

"I will," Ty said.

"Ty, no," Mom said. "Winnie was kidding."

"Actually, Mom—"

"She was kidding," Mom repeated.

Sandra cleared her throat. "One: baked beans make you toot, not green beans."

"Blah-bitty-blah," I said. "And two?"

She shook her head. *"Oy."*

The next day, the two fifth grade classes got together to draw names for Secret Santas. I loved Secret Santas almost as much as I loved Christmas, so I hoped I would draw Amanda's name, or Chantelle's. But I knew I probably wouldn't, and I was right. The folded-up piece of paper I drew from the bag said "Mindy."

I read it silently and thought, *Huh*. Mindy was new this year, she was in Mrs. Tompkins's class, and she was best friends with Katie Jacobson. She hadn't found me amusing when I pretended to be a mad scientist at the World of Coke. That was pretty much all I knew about Mindy, and it didn't add up to a lot.

Well, that's okay, I told myself, folding the paper back up so no one could peek. By being Mindy's Secret Santa, I'd get to know her better. Presto-magico!

I spent a lot of time on Mindy's gift. First I bought an awesome plastic container that I'd spotted in an odd little store at Peachtree Battle Shopping Center. That might sound boring—a plastic container—but this one wasn't boring at all. It was a transparent pale pink rectangle, with crisp edges that begged to be touched. The top fourth of the rectangle was the lid, and when the lid was pulled it off, it made an awesome *swicking* sound. I took the lid on and off a zillion times just to hear that sound.

The container by itself was cool, but I made it even cooler with puff paint. I used fancy lettering to write Mindy's name diagonally down one side, and then to add more flair, I added a buzzing bumblebee and painted wavy lines by its wings to show that it was on the move.

When I painted the bumblebee, I guess I wasn't really thinking holiday-ish thoughts—or maybe I wasn't thinking, period. Because what did bumblebees have to do with Christmas or Hanukkah or whatever holiday the Rasta-whatever-ians celebrated?

But a bumblebee was what flew into my brain as I sat there wondering what to draw, and so a bumblebee it was. A bumblebee with a big chubby stinger. Then I filled the whole container with miniature Reese's cups. It was tricky, because of course I wanted the Reese's cups to fill the entire rectangle, not just the part of the rectangle that was below the lid. I invented a creak-crack quick-pop-one-in SLAM! technique that worked pretty well, though, and I filled that baby up. *Mmmm-mmm.*

I knew that when Mindy popped the lid off for the first time, Reese's cups would spill out in a flood of gold foil. That was okay. It would just add to the fun!

We had our actual gift exchange on the last day before Christmas break. The kids in Mrs. Tompkins's class filed into our room and dropped their wrapped presents off at Ms. Meyers's desk, where our presents were already stacked. Then they found seats on the floor, and everyone was chatty and full of high spirits. I spotted Mindy and bounced in my seat. She was going to *love* her present. Hee hee!

Once everyone was settled down—or as settled down as we were going to get—Ms. Meyers selected the presents one by one, checked the tags, and called kids up to open them. My name was called before Mindy's was, and I skip-hopped to the front of the room. Ms. Meyers handed me a shiny blue cookie tin with reindeers on it, and I pried the top off to find a mountain of homemade potato latkes.

"From Maxine," said a slip of paper. I squealed and said, "Oh, Maxine, thank you thank you thank you!"

Maxine looked happy. "My mom says just microwave them, and they'll be fine."

I took a chomp out of one and made an I'm-in-heaven face. "Okay, but they're already great. I like them cold!"

After that, I munched on potato latkes and waited for Mindy's name to be called. Finally it was, and Mindy went to the front of the room. She was wearing an all-white dress with white fur (probably fake) around the collar and the cuffs of her sleeves. She was very fancy compared to me in my normal old jeans and a Dr Pepper shirt. She was very fancy compared to everybody, actually. But there was nothing wrong with fancy!

"For you," Ms. Meyers said, presenting Mindy with her gift. I'd wrapped it very creatively. I'd covered the container with brown paper cut from a grocery bag. Then I traced my hands on a piece of orange construction paper and cut the handprints out. I glued the orange handprints on top of the wrapped-in-brown box, making them stick up like reindeer antlers. I drew eyes and a mouth on the reindeer's face, and for the nose, I glued on a cotton ball that I'd colored red. It was Rudolph! It was adorable!

Mindy, however, seemed wary as she accepted my reindeer-wrapped gift from Ms. Meyers. Maybe she thought that was the whole present, a fake reindeer head.

"Open it!" I called, hoping to help her realize that she could open it, that the reindeer head was just an amazing wrapping job.

"From Winnie," Mindy said, fingering the tag. She glanced around the room, and I waved and bounced in my seat. She tore off the brown paper and examined the personalized container of Reese's cups. She had to use both hands because of how heavy it was.

"Awwww! That's so cute!" Chantelle said.

I grinned.

"You lucked out," David told Mindy. He turned to me. "Man, Winnie, I wish you'd drawn my name."

My grin grew wider.

Mindy, on the other hand, didn't crack a smile.

"Thanks," she said flatly. She returned to her spot on the carpet and set the container beside her, while up front, Ms. Meyers gathered the remains of Rudolph the Wrapping-Paper Reindeer and threw the scraps in the trash. Later, when Ms. Meyers called out the next kid's name, I saw Mindy nudge the container farther away. She didn't even want it near her.

I was bewildered. Did I do something wrong? Misspell her name? Was she a Rasta-whatever-ian, and Rasta-whatever-ians didn't believe in candy?

During lunch, I gathered my courage and walked over to her. She was sitting at a table with Katie Jacobson. It took a long time for her to notice me, but finally she glanced up and said, "Yes?"

My mouth fell open, but no words came out. I guess I'd expected her to say "Hi" or "Want to sit down?" or "Omigosh, I *love* the container you made. I just get really shy about speaking in public."

She didn't. She simply looked at me as if she were . . .
I don't know . . . a snooty saleslady at Macy's, and I was a
pesky little kid asking for perfume samples.

Katie laughed. It was an ugly laugh. A through-her-nose
laugh.

"I was, um, just wondering if you like your present?" I
said. As I spoke, my voice went up and up.

Mindy sighed. She fished something out from between
her teeth with her tongue, grabbed it with her thumb and
index finger, and wiped it on her napkin. Tilting her head,
she said, "Do you want the truth or a lie?"

"What?" I said. My cheeks got warm, because who said
things like that? People didn't say things like that. Kids,
especially, didn't say things like that.

I should have turned around and walked away. Instead,
I was so flustered that I clasped my hands behind my back
and stammered, "I guess . . . the truth?"

"No," she said, as in, *no, she didn't like my present*. In a
monotone, she ticked off reasons why. "I'm allergic to pea-
nuts, which means I'm allergic to peanut butter, too. The
container is tacky. Your handwriting is, like, *so* babyish, and
I hate the color pink."

Kids at nearby tables had realized something was going
on. They'd stopped talking so they could hear.

Katie elbowed Mindy. "The bee," she said.

"Oh, right," Mindy said. "And that . . . *bumblebee*? Is that
what it's supposed to be?"

I was rooted to the floor. I couldn't move.

"It looks like a turd," Mindy pronounced.

The word *turd* made kids laugh. I wasn't sure how many, but it sounded like lots. All I could think was, *It does not. It has wings. It has stripes. There are wavy lines to show that it's on the move.*

Katie's ugly nose-laugh sounded as if it was coming from underwater. So did Mindy's dismissal.

"You can go now," she informed me, and like a robot, I turned and left.

When I walked past my own table, Amanda and Chantelle glanced at each other in alarm. I saw them through a film of waiting-to-spill tears.

"Winnie?" Amanda said.

She and Chantelle shoved back their seats and trailed me out of the lunchroom. In the hall, they flanked my sides to keep me safe, because I was crying by then. Not noisily. Stonily, although on the inside, I'd crumbled to dust.

"What happened?" Amanda said when we got to the girls' room. It was empty except for us. I went into the far stall, and Amanda and Chantelle crowded in with me.

"It was Mindy, wasn't it?" Chantelle said. "She wasn't very nice when she opened your present."

"What did she say to you?" Amanda demanded. She put her arm around me. "What did she do to make you cry?"

I told them. Amanda's lips formed an "O" of dismay, and Chantelle huffed and said, "How *rude*!"

They took turns trying to make me feel better, telling me that Mindy was a jerk, the present I gave her was awesome, and that nobody heard the "turd" remark except *maybe* the kids sitting right near Mindy and Katie.

Amanda told me that Mindy's parents were divorced, and so were Katie's, and that was the only reason they were friends. Chantelle said she overheard Mrs. Jacobs, the assistant principal, tell a parent that Mindy wasn't "a good fit" for Trinity, and that once Mindy had been sent to the office for calling someone a donkey hole.

"She is *not* someone whose opinion you need to care about," she said. By then, we'd all slid to the floor and were sitting with our knees bent and our legs squished up toward our chests. "I mean it, Winnie."

"She was so mean," I whispered. "It's like . . . she *wanted* to embarrass me. Why would anybody do that?"

Amanda, Chantelle, and I looked at one another. None of us had an answer.

Chantelle wiped the lost expression off her face. Shifting her features around, she said, "Well, we've *all* had our embarrassing moments. Remember when Ms. Katcher thought I was a boy?"

Amanda winced. Mrs. Katcher was our teacher in third grade, and on the first day of school, she called Chantelle "Robert."

"Ms. Katcher was crazy," I said, sniffling.

"She was," Amanda agreed. "Just because you had short hair, that meant you had to be a boy?"

Chantelle lifted her eyebrows. "That's what I'm saying. Em*barr*assing."

"What about the time I got trapped in the bathroom?" Amanda said. "In this very stall?"

I blinked. I'd forgotten all about that, but sure enough, this was the very stall I'd crawled under when Amanda couldn't make the lock unstick.

"I was *so* embarrassed, but you rescued me," Amanda said.

"What about the time you got that staple stuck in your tooth?" Chantelle said to me.

Amanda pressed the back of her hand to her mouth to hide her smile.

"Ha ha," I said. I'd eaten a caramel, and it glued itself to my back tooth. I tried to pry it out with a staple, only to get the staple stuck up there, too.

"You couldn't close your mouth," Chantelle said. "You were afraid you'd jam it in farther."

Amanda widened her jaw as well as her eyes. "You alked ike iss," she said, keeping her top teeth from touching the bottom ones.

My lips twitched.

Amanda let her mouth go back to normal. "*I* had to pull it out. It was covered with spit."

"Yes. Well. These things happen." I tried to sound lofty, but failed.

"Exactly," Chantelle said. She put her hand on my knee.

"You know what, though?" Amanda said. "With the caramel, and the staple? That was your own fault."

I swiveled my head and made a face at her. "Thanks."

"No, I just mean that was all you. You embarrassed yourself."

"And again I say thanks."

She knocked her leg against mine. "You know what I'm saying. Just now, with Mindy, I *know* you were embarrassed—"

"I would have been, too. Anyone would have been," Chantelle piped up.

"Yeah," Amanda said. "But in *reality*"—she looked at me hard—"she embarrassed herself."

"Out of rudeness," Chantelle said.

"Extreme rudeness," Amanda said. "Don't you let her matter, Winnie. Don't you *dare*."

My chest loosened. Even scrunched up in the bathroom with Amanda and Chantelle, I no longer felt small and insignificant, which was how Mindy had made me feel. Instead, I felt . . . blessed.

"Okay," I said. I smiled at my friends. "Thanks."

We sat for a few moments.

"Should we go back?" Chantelle said.

"I guess we should," Amanda said.

I didn't want to, but then I remembered Maxine's mom's potato latkes, waiting for me at my desk.

"I have potato latkes!" I proclaimed loudly.

Chantelle put her hands over her ears. "Ow."

"That was random," Amanda said, giggling.

"Let's go," I said, and the three of us scrambled to our feet. Nobody bonked her head, nobody stepped on someone else's toes, and nobody got locked in or fell in the toilet.

It was a Christ-nukkah-whatever-ian miracle.

January

January first was a day for reflection. It was the first day of a brand-new year, and that was a big deal. It wasn't as big of a deal as my birthday—which was in two months and ten days!!!—but still. New Year's Day was the exact right day for sitting down and making plans for who I wanted to be. In other words, it was the exact right day for writing down my New Year's resolutions.

I got out my spanking new journal, which Santa had put in my stocking, and uncapped one of my spanking new fruit-scented gel pens, which Sandra had wrapped up and put under the tree for me. Good ol' Sandra. My gift to her was a pale blue baby doll shirt that said, *Shalom, y'all!* She loved it, which I knew because she darted to the bathroom and put it on right that second. It looked really pretty with her eyes.

I opened my journal to the first page. It was blank and inviting, a promise waiting to be filled. I gripped my pen—I'd chosen Very Berry Blackberry—and inhaled the tang of its sparkly purple ink. *Yum.*

And now there was nothing left to do except write those resolutions down. Only . . . where to start?

I knew from experience that when it came to writing, thinking too long about something was the kiss of death. I imagined a black blob floating over to a stick-figure girl and saying, *Pucker up, sweetie!* And then, *SPLAT!* The stick-figure girl would fall down dead, limbs splayed and X's over her eyes.

That was no way to start a new year.

So I got that pen moving. I didn't let myself worry about whether what I wrote was dumb or wrong or embarrassing, because it was *my* journal. Plus, wasn't I allowed to be dumb, wrong, and embarrassing sometimes? Everybody did things that were dumb, wrong, and embarrassing sometimes, just like Chantelle said.

Well, hellooooooooo, me! I wrote. It's January 1st, the first day of an entire new year. An entire new going-to-be-GREAT year! And the reason it's going to be great is because I'm going to MAKE it great. Yep, you heard it here first, folks!

So with that as my goal, I hereby resolve:

• That I won't let a certain girl named MINDY get under my skin.

I didn't exactly intend to put that resolution down first, but getting Mindy out of my head and onto the paper flooded me with so much relief that I was glad I did. I guess I'd been worrying about Mindy more than I realized, even over Christmas break.

But I didn't want to let Mindy matter to me, and so I wouldn't. *La la la. Mindy who?*

What next?

I bit my lip, then kept writing.

• I won't worry about other things, either. For example, bees or rules or—dun dun dun—the Bathroom Lady. Be gone, Bathroom Lady! Be gone!

There was something else that went along with that, so I decided I might as well put it down, too.

• I will also stop flushing the toilet.

Wait, that wasn't right. Do-over!

• ~~I will also stop flushing the toilet.~~ I will no longer not not flush the toilet. In fact, I WILL FLUSH THE TOILET <u>EVERY</u> TIME I USE IT. That is an order, young lady. Got it?

The truth was that I'd gotten better about the Bathroom Lady, meaning that as long as I didn't think about her, I was fine. But when I did think about her . . . alone in the downstairs bathroom, say . . . or late at night when suddenly and desperately I had to use the bathroom . . .

I shuddered. The surest way to make myself need to use the bathroom was to tell myself I didn't, just as the surest way to creep myself out about the Bathroom Lady was to tell myself not, under any circumstances, to think about pruney claws or just plain claws, or even just plain prunes.

So don't, I told myself.

Can't you see I'm trying? I replied. *Sheesh!*

The problem was that I had a very good imagination, and having a good imagination had its pluses and its minuses. On the plus side, when I dreamed, I dreamed BIG. Finding a magic wish-granting penny? Stumbling on a secret system of tunnels beneath our house? Becoming pen pals with Al Roker's daughter? Why not? Those things *could* happen. They could *totally* happen.

But when my imagination turned toward not-so-happy topics . . . well, it was bad. I didn't even want to think of examples, although here they came just the same: Being kidnapped! Biting my own tongue off! Biting someone *else's* tongue off! And once a thought popped into my brain, it was nearly impossible to make it leave—just like the Bathroom Lady, for example. Mom called it getting trapped in a bad thought pattern. Sandra called it obsessing. I didn't call it anything, but I didn't like it.

What Mom and Dad and Sandra didn't understand was that I didn't mean to let my imagination run wild. I didn't on purpose think, *Ooo! Hot dogs for dinner, yay! I JUST HOPE THEY DON'T CLOG TY'S THROAT THE WAY THE BLACK RUBBER STOPPER CLOGS UP THE KITCHEN SINK, BECAUSE THEN HE COULD STOP BREATHING AND TURN PURPLE AND DIE!*

Wait. What did hot dogs have to do with my New Year's resolutions? Nothing . . . except that eating animal intestines was seriously gross, so maybe I should resolve to not eat hot dogs anymore.

Except hot dogs were also seriously delicious, so maybe my resolution should be not to think about how hot dogs are made.

Yes. Excellent solution.

• I will never again think about how hot dogs are made, I scribbled.

Then I groaned, remembering how hard it was to NOT think about something once I'd already made the mistake of thinking about it.

• I won't think about it on purpose, that is. And if I'm in a group of people and the topic comes up, I will walk away. That's right. I will WALK. AWAY. And the moral of this story is?

Bring it on, New Year! Let the good times roll!

I made the exclamation point at the end of that sentence big and bold, and then I capped my pen and put it down. Then I uncapped it, breathed in its smell one last time, *re*capped it, and put it down for real.

With my resolutions done, it was time to get started on the good times rolling part. I left my bedroom and took a moment to check in on everyone. Sandra was in her room, doing something boring on her laptop. I trotted downstairs, where I found Mom and Dad watching *Masterpiece Theater* in the den. Ty was in there with them, playing with his toy cars and quietly going *vroom, vroom* as he made them race along the floor.

"Hi," I said, waving.

"Hi, Winnie," Mom said. "Want to watch *Pride and Prejudice* with us?"

"No thanks, but thanks for the offer," I said politely. "Bye now!"

Knowing the coast was clear, I tromped down to the basement, where I took hold of a very large cardboard box and dragged it up to the main level of the house. I'd been wanting some alone time with this box ever since Christmas, when Dad had pried it open and pulled out a new lamp to be used in the den. It was a present from Mom.

The box—and the lamp—were as tall as I was, and while Mom and Dad and Sandra had oohed and aahed over the lamp, I'd privately oohed and aahed over the box, considering its many possibilities. Ty had been too busy with a new racetrack gizmo to pay attention to either.

When Mom caught me eyeing the box, she tilted her head and said, "Winnie? This box is not for climbing in."

"I know, I know," I said.

To Dad, she said, "Joel, will you please break it down and take it to the recycling bin after we finish opening presents?"

"Of course, of course," Dad said.

But he didn't. He lugged it to the bottom of the basement staircase and forgot about it. I, however, did not.

I pulled the box into the back hallway and took a break to catch my breath. With it on its side the way it was, I suspected I could scoot all the way in and be totally contained. I tried it, and I was right. I thought about how much Amanda's cat, Sweet Pea, loved to curl up in boxes or baskets or open drawers, and I pretended I was a cat. Then I pretended I was dead, and the box was my coffin.

It worked, until someone came along and kicked the box's side.

"Hey!" I complained, pushing open the top of the box and peering out.

Sandra stood above me. "Move," she said.

"What are you doing here? Go back to your room," I said.

She snorted and stepped over me, deliberately allowing her heel to bang into the cardboard.

"*Hey!* Gentle!" I said.

"Don't worry, I'm fine," she said. She jerked her chin at the storage closet behind me. "I need the hammer out of Dad's toolbox, though, and I need something to step on so I can reach that high." She lifted her foot, as well as her eyebrows. "Mind if I . . . ?"

"Yes, I mind!" I cried, squirming out of the box. "You'd squish it, you big lug. And you'd squish me. And you *don't* need Dad's hammer—you totally made that up, didn't you?"

She laughed and went on her merry way while I stood guard in front of my box. She grabbed a Coke from the kitchen and returned to the back hall.

"Still here?"

"*Bye now,*" I said with narrowed eyes.

She laughed again. "So weird," she said, *fakily* under her breath. But she left, so fine.

I pulled the box to the kitchen, where I could have some privacy. What would be really cool, I decided, would be if I could somehow find a way to be in the box while standing up. Not standing on the floor with the box pulled over me, but actually standing inside the box with my feet on the cardboard bottom and the top of my head inches below the open cardboard flaps.

Hmm. If I climbed onto the kitchen counter, I'd be high enough to lower myself into the box. If I pulled the box over to the edge of the counter, I could hold myself up with my hands and ease myself in, feetfirst. I'd have to tilt the box diagonally, but it would straighten up as I dropped all the way in.

I realized my mistake the instant I let go of the counter. As I dropped into the box, my arms slid up, pinned between my ears and the cardboard sides. The momentum threw my body against the front of the box, and everything tilted forward.

"Ahhh!" I yelled. My forehead smacked the tiled kitchen floor, and the world went dark.

Mom was too embarrassed to take me to the emergency room.

"What would I tell them?" she said, once I came to. "My daughter was pretending to be a lamp, so she jumped feet-first into a box? Anyway, you were only out for a minute. Two minutes, tops."

She pressed a washcloth filled with ice against my head

and readjusted my pillow. Dad had carried me upstairs to my bed during my two minutes of unconsciousness, I'd been told. He was now outside breaking down the box. Ty was with him, helping him jump on it.

"I wasn't pretending to be a lamp," I protested. I lifted my Coke to my lips. I took a tiny sip and put it back on my bedside table.

"Not to mention the fact that it's New Year's Day. The emergency room is probably overflowing with drunks and degenerates."

"So she'd fit right in," Sandra called from her room.

"Eavesdropper!" I called, then winced and wished I hadn't.

Mom shook her head. "What a way to usher in the new year. If the swelling isn't down by morning, I'll take you to Dr. Larson's."

"Can I have another Coke when I finish this one?" I asked.

"No," Sandra called.

"Sandra? Hush," Mom called back. To me, she said, "Absolutely not, and you're lucky you didn't break your nose."

I got to watch movies in bed for the rest of the night. Dad brought up the portable DVD player that we used on long car trips, and Ty snuggled up with me, asking every so often if he could touch my bump. Sandra tracked down Dad's camera and took pictures of it.

"Quit," I said.

"I haven't gotten it from this angle," she said, squeezing onto my bed and taking a picture from below my head.

"Quit!"

"Fine, you big baby." She put the camera on my nightstand, but stayed where she was. "Poor little Nemo," she mused, getting sucked into the movie. "When, oh when, will you realize that you weren't big enough to go out on your own?"

I elbowed her, but not hard. I liked being cuddled up with Ty on one side and Sandra on the other. They were the bread, and I was the cheese. Or the baloney. No, the cheese, just not the *hi-ho the derry-o* sort of cheese, because the one thing I *wasn't* was alone.

"Here you go, sweetie," Mom said, coming in with a fresh ice pack. "Are you feeling any better?"

"A little," I said. "Do you want to watch *Finding Nemo* with us?"

She was about to say no. I saw it on her face. Then she smiled and said, "Sure." Angling her head toward the hall, she called, "Joel! Come up to Winnie's room. We're having family movie night!"

The three of us kids scooched into the middle of my bed, which luckily was a queen-size bed and barely big enough for the whole family. Mom and Dad made up the bookends. I was still in the very middle.

We watched the movie. I cried when Marlin realized Nemo wasn't dead after all, and Mom reached over Ty and gently rubbed the back of my neck. "Oh, Winnie. You've had a rough start to the year, haven't you?"

"Huh?" I said. I was with my whole family, watching a movie *I* picked out. And sure, the ending made me weepy, but in a good way. "Um, if by that you mean the *best* start to the year, then yes."

Mom laughed. "All right, well, I really don't know what you just said. But if you're happy, I'm happy."

"I'm happy," I said. "Anyway, every day is a new day, not just *this* particular day which happens to be called New Year's Day."

"You lost me," Mom said.

"Just nod and say, 'Yes, Winnie. We love you, Winnie,'" Sandra said in a mock-whisper. "She got hit in the head, you know. In a box. *All by herself.*"

I whapped her. "Shush up, you."

"I *do* love you, Winnie," Ty said. He yawned. "And I'm glad you're not a shark, even though some sharks turn out to be nice."

"I love you, too, Ty. And you and you and you," I said, looking at Mom, Dad, and Sandra in turn.

Sandra rolled her eyes.

I rolled mine back at her. "And all I mean is that no matter what, we can always start fresh tomorrow."

February

I n February, Mindy started a secret club. A *mean* secret club. Every morning, she and Katie picked a special friend for the day. First, the girl they chose had to be inspected: her clothes had to be the right kind of clothes, her hair had to be in an acceptable style, her personality had to meet some mysterious standard that only Mindy and Katie understood.

If the girl scored at least a seven out of ten, then she passed the inspection, and she got to eat lunch with Mindy and Katie and whisper with Mindy and Katie and torment people on the playground with Mindy and Katie.

Often they tormented Dinah Devine.

"She still wets her pants," Mindy said loudly in the lunchroom last week. "I can smell it."

"I feel sorry for her," Katie said. But she didn't mean it.

On the Dinah-wets-her-pants day, Louise was their special buddy. She blinked nervously and said, "Me too," and Mindy and Katie laughed. It was unclear who they were laughing at.

More often, however, they tormented *me*. They claimed I sneezed on my sandwich and ate it anyway. They claimed I dug an eye booger out of my eye and ate that, too. They called me "Lint," because lint clung to things and was annoying. But I didn't cling to things, especially them. They had just decided I was the enemy, that's all. Or the target, like in a game of darts, and their words and eye-rolls and snickers were the darts.

But Mindy made me cry one time and one time only: the time she was so mean about the Secret Santa present I gave her. I hadn't cried since then, and I wasn't going to.

That didn't mean their teasing didn't hurt.

On the outside, I pretended to be brave Winnie who wasn't scared of anything: not toilets, not outside garbage cans, not the Bathroom Lady, and not Mindy. But on the inside, I *wanted* to cry. On the inside I felt like I was three going on four, like Ty had been when frilly Erica was mean to him at the pool, instead of ten coming up fast on eleven.

One cold morning, Amanda dashed up and pulled me to the corner of the room.

"You're not going to believe this. It's *bad*," she said.

"What?" I said.

"No, Winnie, it's *really* bad. It's . . . Chantelle."

"Is she sick?"

Amanda shook her head. "Worse. Mindy and Katie picked her to be their friend for the day."

My gut clenched. "What?!"

"I know, but they did. And Chantelle, she . . ." Amanda pressed her lips together. "She said yes."

"But . . . but . . ."

"I know," Amanda said again.

"She herself said how rude Mindy is. She *knows* how rude Mindy is!"

Amanda's expression was bleak. "I know," she said for the third and final time. "I just thought I'd warn you."

I felt sick all day. When recess came around, I felt so sick I thought I might actually throw up.

I grabbed Amanda and said, "Come on, let's go swing."

Maybe if I was swooping up and down through the air, I told myself, then Mindy couldn't get to me.

Wrong.

"Here they come," Amanda said from the swing beside me.

I didn't want to look. I couldn't help *but* look. My head turned on its own to take in their cocky saunter across the playground: Mindy, Katie, and—yes—Chantelle. Chantelle looked pretty and put together, like she always did, but she also looked . . . different. I couldn't put my finger on how.

"Why?" I whispered, meaning why why *why* would Chantelle do this, when the person she was doing it to was me?

"I have no idea," Amanda said.

"Maybe . . . maybe they won't be mean this time. Chantelle wouldn't let them be *mean*, would she?"

Amanda didn't respond.

They arrived with linked arms. Chantelle wouldn't meet my gaze.

"Well, if it isn't Lint," Mindy said. She smiled. "Girls, say hi to Lint."

"Hi, Lint," Katie said. Her tone was perfectly friendly. She even gave a little wave.

"My name's not—" I broke off. What was the point?

"Chantelle?" Mindy prompted.

"Chantelle, don't," Amanda said to her.

"You don't want Chantelle to say hi to her friend?" Mindy said.

"How rude," Katie said.

Mindy hip-bumped Chantelle, and Chantelle stumbled because she'd been holding herself so rigidly. *That* was what was different about her. Chantelle, usually as fluid and graceful as water, was as stiff as a crayon. A waxy, expressionless crayon.

I willed her to just look at me and see that it was *me*, but she didn't. She stared at the ground and said, "Hi."

"Hi who?" Mindy prodded.

Don't, I willed her.

With a crayon's lifeless energy, Chantelle said, "Hi, Lint."

Shame rose up in me, and all at once I needed to stop swinging. I *had* to stop swinging, because I'd felt ill all along, but now there was a real chance that my stomach would turn itself inside out, and up would come my breakfast plus my morning snack.

If I threw up in front of Mindy, I would die. I'd have to drop out of Trinity and switch schools. I'd have to move to a new state, or Canada.

"I am *so* disappointed in you, Chantelle," Amanda said, loud and clear and brave. She hopped off her swing. "Come on, Winnie. Let's go do something fun. Let's go find the *nice* people."

I was dizzy with gratitude, and I jumped off poorly, lurching forward and going down hard.

"Ow," I said, unable not to.

Mindy snorted. From above me, her words pelted my sprawled figure like rocks. "Do you know what you're like, Winnie? You're like a flea on a dog's back that I just can't get rid of, no matter how hard I try."

I pushed myself to my knees. I had to. I rose unsteadily to my feet and made myself say the words I was thinking. "Does that make you the dog?"

Mindy's eyes widened. Then they narrowed, turning to flint. She stepped closer. "What did you just say?"

Amanda moved beside me and took my hand.

"Well, if I'm a flea"—my voice wobbled, but I pressed on—"then that makes you the dog. Right?"

Mindy's nostrils flared. "You're calling me a *dog?*"

I shrugged. *I* wasn't calling her a dog. She was calling herself a dog.

"Take it back," she said. She got up in my face. *"Take. It. Back."*

Her breath smelled like honey. Splotches of red mottled her skin, and I could see every fleck of color in her eyes. I'd thought they were just brown, but there was gold mixed in as well. On her left iris, above the pupil, a particularly large slash of gold stood out.

She slapped me.

All thoughts flew from my mind, replaced first by shock and then by pain. Then came a tunneling-in of time like nothing I'd ever experienced, even when I fell over in the lamp box and was knocked unconscious. Everything was bright. Everything happened slowly.

Amanda gasped. She slapped Mindy, or tried to, but Mindy's hand flew up and caught her wrist, twisting it until Amanda cried out.

"Let her go!" I yelled. I threw myself at Mindy, knocking her to the ground. Dimly, I heard Chantelle say, "Amanda, are you okay?" Katie said something, too, but I didn't know what, and I didn't care.

I pinned Mindy's wrists to the ground and drove my knee into her hip. She kneed me in the gut. When that didn't work, she squirmed beneath me and dug her fingernails into my skin.

I clenched my jaw, but I didn't punch her, or spit at her,

or any number of other things I could have done. I also didn't release her, because *nobody* hurts my friend.

"You guys, the teachers are coming!" I heard. Hands pulled at me urgently. "Winnie, get up. If they catch you fighting . . ."

A second set of hands tugged at me, and Amanda's face appeared upside down in my line of vision. "Winnie, hurry. *Please.*"

And then—*swoosh*. Time returned to normal. The playground teemed with noise. I pushed my weight into Mindy one last time, and then I let her go and rolled off her. I breathed heavily, clasping my arms around my shins.

Mindy sat up. A twig clung to her hair. Her gold-flecked eyes were animal eyes, cold and flat.

"You are so dead," she told me. "You're going to get expelled, you know."

"No way, Mindy," Amanda said, fast and slow. "*You* slapped Winnie. So if anyone gets in trouble, it'll be you, because you started it."

"Says who?" Mindy demanded. She gestured at Katie and Chantelle. "I've got witnesses. Three against two."

"You think you can just *lie*?" Amanda said. "On top of everything else?"

Ms. Meyers was almost to us. Mr. Hutchinson, one of the sixth grade teachers, was close behind.

Amanda grabbed Chantelle's elbow, pulling her away from Katie. Chantelle came willingly, and my brain registered a detail that I hadn't fully processed.

Two people pulled me off Mindy. Two people wanted to save me from getting in trouble.

"Chantelle is with us," Amanda stated. "Right, Chantelle?"

Chantelle gulped and bobbed her head. She looked at me—finally—and she was no longer a crayon, because crayons didn't have eyes that welled with tears. *"Sorry,"* she whispered miserably.

Amanda helped me get to my feet.

"We choose Winnie," she said, putting her arm around me.

"Yeah," Chantelle said.

My lower lip trembled. I wiggled my fingers at Chantelle to say, *Get over here, you stinky-poo-poo-head*, and I pulled her into our hug.

"Girls?" Ms. Meyers said. Her tone was concerned and dangerous at the same time. Mr. Hutchinson joined her. He was *tall*. Usually he was a joking-around kind of teacher, but not right now.

"We're fine," Amanda said.

Ms. Meyers turned to me, lifting her eyebrows.

"We were, uh, playing cats and dogs," I said. "I guess maybe we got a little too rough?"

"I'll say," Ms. Meyers said. She glanced at Katie, and then at Mindy, who was sitting sullenly on the flattened grass. "Do either of you have anything to add?"

"No, ma'am," Katie muttered. Katie never said "ma'am," so it was weird.

"Mindy?" Mr. Hutchinson said.

She shook her head. She didn't look up.

Ms. Meyers folded her arms over her chest. "Well, how about this. How about you all promise not to play that game anymore. Agreed?"

"Agreed," Amanda, Chantelle, and I said as one.

"Agreed," Katie mumbled.

Ms. Meyers waited, and Mindy rolled her eyes.

"Agreed." Under her breath, she added, *"Duh."*

Ms. Meyers lectured us about taking care of ourselves, our friends, and our school, and after that, the group broke up. Mindy and Katie went to the opposite side of the playground, and Amanda, Chantelle, and I went to the swing set. It felt good to pump and move and feel the air lift my hair.

After a minute of silence, I turned to Chantelle and said, "You're not really a stinky-poo-poo-head."

She scrunched her brow, and I remembered I'd only called her that in my head.

I backpedaled. "I mean . . . well, I *didn't* mean—"

"No, don't," she said. She was going back and forth, and so was I, but I could hear her just fine. "I am a poo-poo-head. I don't know what I was thinking, Winnie. I'm so so sorry."

Everything was still strange. I was slowly starting to feel better, though.

"I forgive you," I said with a quick hitch of my shoulders.

"You don't have to."

"I want to." *Mostly*, I thought. And I suspected that after a little more time passed, I fully would.

"Let's just swing," I said. I leaned back, pointed my toes, and pulled hard on the chain, soaring into the wide, blue sky.

March

S ometimes I lounged around in bed after I woke up,
just to enjoy being happy for a while. Today was the
perfect day for this, because it was a Saturday, which meant
no school. Also it was bright and cheerful outside, which I
knew because of the stripe of buttery light stretching into
my room from beneath my blinds. But the biggest reason
why today was a perfect day for soaking up the awesome-
ness of being alive? BECAUSE MY BIRTHDAY WAS ONLY
A SIX DAYS AWAY!

Yep. This coming Friday was March eleventh, and on
March eleventh, I would be eleven years old. It was so so so
so cool. So cool! Mom had said I could have a slumber party,
and I'd sent out invitations to Amanda, Chantelle, Louise,
Karen, and—because Mom made me, big surprise—Dinah
Devine. Every one of them said they could come. Yay!

I did *not* invite Mindy. But! BUT! I couldn't have invited
her even if I'd wanted to, because Mindy had moved to
Florida. *Ha ha ha ha ha*!

She left last week. Boo hoo . . . NOT! Only I knew I

shouldn't be gloaty about it, because although it was excellent news for me, I guess it wasn't so excellent for Mindy.

I knew this because eventually I confessed to Mom about beating Mindy up. Or rather, about starting to beat her up . . . and *wanting* to keep on going. I twisted my hands together as I told her all the gory details, until finally she reached over and took my hands in her own.

"Winnie, stop," she said.

I swallowed. I felt dizzy knowing how disappointed she must be in me.

"I want to tell you something, and I want you to listen, all right?" she said.

I looked at my lap.

"I want you to listen to me *and* look at me. I'm not going to say anything bad."

I lifted my eyes. She didn't look mad or disappointed. She *did* look serious.

"Why didn't you tell me about Mindy earlier?" she asked.

"I don't know," I said. "Because I kept hoping it would get better?"

"Oh, Winnie."

"And also you would have said, 'Oh, Winnie,' like you just did. Like I'd let you down."

Mom's eyes teared up. I felt my own eyes get bigger when I saw that—*I* could make Mom cry?—but there was something inside of me that felt happy about that, too. Not *happy* . . . well, *maybe* happy . . . or more just relieved to be finally getting it off my chest.

"You would have said to confront Mindy," I went on, "or to tell Ms. Meyers. And if I said I didn't want to tell Ms. Meyers, you would have said, '*Oh, Winnie.* You can't be afraid to talk to your teacher.'"

"I wouldn't have said that," Mom insisted.

I lifted my eyebrows.

"Would I have?"

I nodded.

"*Oh, Winnie,*" she said, and we both laughed a little, because she'd used the exact tone I used, and not even on purpose, I don't think. "Sweetheart. You have *never* let me down."

"What about when I don't put my dishes in the dishwasher? What about when I forget to say 'excuse me' when I burp?"

"You *burp*?" she said, placing her hand over her heart. "*You,* my darlingest Winnie?"

"Very funny," I said.

Mom studied me, and I sensed that she was really and truly seeing me. "Winnie, everyone burps."

"Ha! You admitted it!" I said, because whenever Dad or Ty tooted or burped or acted too much like gross boys, Mom claimed that *she* never did anything so unladylike. "*Ha!*"

She allowed herself a small smile. Then she went back

to being solemn. "But what Mindy was doing—picking a friend for a day, doing inspections of how certain girls looked . . ."

"Calling me a flea."

"Calling you a flea." She shook her head. "You are *not* a flea, Winifred Perry. I hope you know that."

"Woof," I said, so that I was a dog instead. Then I remembered about the flea being on a dog's back, and I changed my tune. "I mean, *me-o-o-w.*"

She ruffled my hair. "You are a *goof.* That's what you are."

"I know. Can I get a kitten, by the way? Please-oh-please with champagne on top?"

"What Mindy did wasn't nice," Mom said. "And sweetie, you shouldn't have had to deal with it on your own. A problem like that is too big for a ten-year-old."

"I'm almost eleven," I reminded her.

"It's too big for an eleven-year-old," she said.

Wowza, I thought. An amazed feeling made my skin tingle, because I *had* dealt with it, and I'd dealt with it even *before* I was eleven.

"Remembering to feed your fish, now that's a problem a ten-year-old can tackle," Mom said.

"I don't have any fish."

"But if you did."

"I'd rather have a kitten."

"Yes, I know."

"I would totally remember to feed a kitten, if I had one."

"Yes, now *shhh*. Remembering to do your spelling home-work, that is also a problem a ten-year-old can handle."

I made a face. Spelling homework was boring.

"But when someone bullies you like that—and that's what Mindy was doing, Winnie—you need to get a grown-up's help. A mom's help, or a dad's help. That's why we're here. We love you *so much*, Winnie."

I felt naked in the face of all that love. Not naked as if I wasn't wearing any clothes, because of course I was wearing clothes. But . . . teensy-tinesy, like a helpless little baby? Not that I was a little baby!

I think what Mom was trying to say, though, was that she and Dad would take care of me even if I *was* as helpless as a baby. That I didn't always have to be their "big girl." I *was* their big girl—not as big as Sandra, but big just the same—but I think Mom was saying that I could be their little girl every so often, and she and Dad would love me just the same.

"I love you, too," I said. My voice was wobbly, and I blinked.

Mom pushed my hair behind my ear. "And while I may *occasionally* scold you for not putting your dishes in the dishwasher, you are *not* a disappointment to me. Never. You don't let me down, Winnie. You lift me up. Don't you know that?"

I nodded. I liked what she was saying, but it was embarrassing, too. "Can we talk about kittens again?"

She got up and said, "I'm going to call Mrs. Jacobs. She needs to know what's going on, especially if Mindy is treating other girls like she treated you."

So she did. Afterward, she told me what Mrs. Jacobs said, and I learned that there were sadnesses in Mindy's life just like there were in everybody's lives. Apparently Mindy's mom, who lived in Atlanta, didn't want Mindy anymore, and so she was sending Mindy to Florida to live with her dad.

That wasn't exactly how Mom put it, but that was the gist of it. She said I had to put that information "in the vault," which meant I wasn't allowed to tell anyone.

I tried feeling bad for Mindy, but mainly I was just glad she was gone. And the fact that she left before my birthday was an extra-special bonus.

My lazy morning came to an end when Dad and his buddy Elmo came up to my room to install a floor-to-ceiling bookcase in my room. It was supposedly an early birthday present, since I loved books so much. I didn't think furniture counted as a birthday present, but I was excited nonetheless.

Dad told me to skedaddle so that he and Elmo could do their "man's work."

"Will you call when you're done?" I said. "The very *minute* you're done?"

Dad promised he would, and three-and-a-half hours later—after lots of banging, cursing, and pizza-eating—he called for me to come see.

I left Ty and Sandra to finish the *SpongeBob* marathon on their own and flew upstairs.

"OMIGOSH, IT ROCKS!" I squealed. I took in my new bookcase, which was beautiful and empty and just waiting to be filled with delicious books. Then I took in the rest of my room, because it was different now. My dresser was against the opposite wall, and my bed was where my dresser used to be. The bookcase stood proudly in the bed's old spot.

"You rearranged things," I said.

"A section of the crown molding had to be removed for the bookcase to fit," Dad explained. "Do you like it?"

"Are you kidding?" I said. I flung myself on Dad and wrapped my legs around his waist, because whether I was a big girl or a little girl, it would always be fun to tackle him. "I *love* it and adore it, and you are the best daddy in the whole entire world!"

"I'm glad," he said. "Now let go, sweetie." He tried to pry me off him, but I had legs of steel, and I knew to hook my ankles behind his back and lock them together.

From over his shoulder, I checked out my room some more. With the bookcase adding to the decor, it was like I'd been given a whole new room. It was less little-girlish, which was perfect, since I'd be eleven in six short days.

Six days. Whoa.

A year ago, my room had been completely different—and so had I. Well, kind of. *Hmm.* Was I the same Winnie or a different Winnie? Was there any way to know?

I thought back to my scary haunted house party, and I smiled at the memory of ten-year-old me. Then another memory popped into my mind, the memory of little me balancing a chair on my bed and slipping a letter to myself into the gap between the molding and the wall.

But my new bookcase was where my bed used to be. My gaze traveled to the bookcase, and I breathed a sigh of relief, because the molding to either side of the bookcase was still there, *including* the bit where my hiding spot was. *Whew.*

I dropped free of Dad. The sudden weight change made him stumble.

"Hey, Dad?" I said.

"Yes, Winnie?"

"Would you put me on your shoulders, please?"

"Why?"

"Just because. Please?"

He sighed and got down on one knee. "Climb on."

I climbed on top of him and got situated. With a groan, he stood up.

"Now take me over to my bookcase."

He lumbered across the room.

"Closer, and to the right."

He got right up next to the wall. Even on top of Dad, I

wasn't tall enough to look down into my hiding spot. I *was* tall enough to pat the molding, and then the space behind the molding, where the hollow space should have been. Only there was no hollow space. It was gone.

A panicky feeling tried to latch on to my insides.

"Winnie, what are you looking for?" Dad said.

"There was a hole," I said. "There was a hole up near the top of the wall, and I hid something in it!"

With me on his shoulders, Dad backed away from the wall.

"Wait!" I cried, but he was already lifting me up and over him.

He sat me on the floor. "Honey, we filled in that gap with caulk."

"Did you check first to see if anything was in there?"

"We did, and there wasn't."

I turned to Elmo, whose expression confirmed it.

"But I put a letter in there! And also a candy bar!"

"A *candy* bar?" Dad said.

"They couldn't have disappeared," I insisted. "And don't try to tell me roaches got it, or termites, because something would have been left."

Dad scratched the back of his neck. "Huh. If what you're saying is true, then that's strange, I admit. Elmo?"

"The ceiling joists must have shifted, and the gap between the molding and the wall grew bigger," Elmo said, as if it were all very simple. "Winnie, your letter and your candy bar must have slipped behind the wall. Then, when the weather turned cold, the gap contracted."

"You're saying the *wall* ate my stuff? Not roaches or squirrels or termites, but the wall?"

"'Ate' isn't the word I'd use, but yes," Elmo said.

"And today you and Dad filled in the gap. For good."

"We don't want drafts," Dad said. "Our heating bill is high enough as it is."

It was a lot to take in. I leaned against the wall—the very wall that ate my letter and candy bar—and slid down until my bottom reached the floor. "I need some alone time, if you don't mind."

"Sure," Dad said. He hesitated. "Are you all right? What did this letter say, if you don't mind my asking?"

"I wrote down all my hopes and dreams," I said. "I wrote them down so I'd remember who I wanted to be." I felt spacey and out of it, because try though I might, I couldn't call up much more than that.

What had *I written???* Something about being awesome . . . ? Something about staying awesome no matter what . . . ?

"You know," Elmo said, pulling me back to the moment, "a wall actually isn't a bad place to store a letter."

I lifted my eyes.

"Think about it. Unless your folks tear the house down—"

"Which we won't," Dad interrupted.

"Then you'll always know where it is. You can't lose a wall, you know what I mean?"

The ghost of a smile flitted through my mind. *You can't lose a wall.*

"You also can't lose your dreams, pumpkin," Dad said. He rumpled my hair so roughly that my whole head moved back and forth like a bell.

Dad and Elmo went downstairs.

I stayed put and thought about the situation.

Would I have chosen for the wall to eat my letter?

No.

Was I given a vote in the matter?

No again.

How*ever* . . .

It *was* pretty cool that the letter I wrote would always be part of our house, just as my hopes and dreams would always be a part of me. The more I got used to the idea, the more I realized what a shiny and sparkly twist of fate it was.

Anyway, so what if I couldn't remember exactly what I'd written down? Maybe people's dreams changed over time, just like people themselves changed. Because people *did* change. I knew that from personal experience. So maybe my dreams had changed, too?

But I was still Winnie. I would always be Winnie, and I would always keep hoping and dreaming, no matter what.

And Dad was right that you didn't lose your dreams just because a hole in the wall was filled in with caulk. Maybe there were a few things I didn't yet know about this world of ours, and maybe—*occasionally*—there were things I even got wrong. Shocking, I know.

But dreams were forever. That I knew for sure.

Growing up is more fun with a friend like Winnie!

Eleven

PB 978-0-14-240346-4
$6.99 ($8.50 CAN)

HC 978-0-525-47165-3
$16.99 ($21.00 CAN)

Twelve

PB 978-0-14-241091-2
$6.99 ($8.50 CAN)

HC 978-0-525-47784-6
$16.99 ($21.00 CAN)

The Winnie Years Journal

HC 978-0-525-42398-0
$8.99 ($10.99 CAN)

Don't miss any of the Winnie Years series . . .

Thirteen

PB 978-0-14-241370-8
$6.99 ($8.50 CAN)

HC 978-0-525-47896-6
$15.99 ($20.00 CAN)

Thirteen Plus One

PB 978-0-14-241901-4
$6.99 ($8.50 CAN)

HC 978-0-525-42222-8
$16.99 ($21.00 CAN)

Turn the page for a preview just for you of Eleven . . .

March

THE THING ABOUT BIRTHDAYS is that everything should go just right, at least on that one day. And so far today has been perfect, even without cupcakes to pass out during lunch. Not in fifth grade, I told Mom. In fourth grade, sure, but not in fifth. The only kid who'd brought birthday cupcakes was Dinah Devine, and that was at the beginning of the year, so she didn't know better. That's one problem with early birthdays: no one knows what'll be cool and what'll be stupid.

March birthdays are better, like mine. And this birthday in particular, because today is March 11, and today I am eleven years old. It'll only happen like this once, which is why it's especially wonderful that everything's been going so well. Waffles for breakfast, crispy but not burned. At school, a heartfelt chorus of "Happy Birthday," with me beaming at the front of the room. (Ignored Alex Plotkin's bit about monkeys and zoos.) And now, back home in our den, I get to hum and bounce on the sofa to my heart's content without Mom putting her hand on my shoulder and telling me to relax. Not that I *could* relax even if I wanted to. Because in ten minutes or possibly less, I'll have arrived at the best part of the entire day. My party!

During art, Amanda and I had planned out the whole evening, from activities to cake to presents. Ms. Straus had let us scoot our chairs together, and we talked while we drew. Lately I've been liking to draw girls hanging by their knees off tree branches, while Amanda tends to sketch cheerleaders doing daring, fantastic jumps.

"I think you should do presents before cake," Amanda had suggested as she shaded in her cheerleader's skirt. "That way people can have time to digest their pizza."

"Plus, that means I'll get to open the presents sooner," I said. I knew that sounded rude, but with Amanda I could say anything.

"What's your top birthday present ever?" she asked. "Your very favorite thing you ever got."

"From my parents or someone else?"

Amanda switched pencils. "I already know your best gift from your parents: your CD player. From someone else."

I claimed the blue pencil and worked on my girl's shorts. "Well, I *love* the heart necklace you gave me last year."

She rolled her eyes like, *go on.*

"Other than that, I'd guess I'd say my crutches." They were old-fashioned wooden crutches with rubber tips, and they were awesome for acting out stories about brave crippled children or amputees. I'd found them when I was helping my aunt Lucy set up for a garage sale, and she let me keep them as a thank-you-slash-early-birthday-present.

"The crutches are great," Amanda acknowledged, "but what I got you this year is even better." She grinned at my expression. "I can't wait until you see!"

I couldn't wait either, which made me think of another terrific thing about March 11. This year it fell on a Friday, which meant I got to have my party on the exact day of my birthday. Last year it fell on a Wednesday, and the following weekend I had a haunted-house birthday even though it obviously wasn't Halloween. Mom made a cake shaped like a ghost, and my sister Sandra dressed up like a witch and stirred a pot of witch's brew down in the basement. It was really a pot of dry ice we got from Baskin-Robbins, but the steam made it look spooky, and Dinah Devine screamed and got the hiccups and had to be taken upstairs. Then my little brother Ty wet his pants and started to cry.

Another good thing: Mom's paying Sandra ten dollars to take Ty to Chuck E. Cheese, his favorite place in the world. He could spend eons there.

From the window, I saw a blue Honda pull into the drive-way. I scrambled off the sofa and called, "Mom, get down here!" I opened the front door and ran to greet Amanda, who was carrying a medium-size box wrapped in bright green paper. "Amanda! Finally!"

Amanda twisted away with her present, which I was trying to wrest free. "Hands off," she said.

"What is it?" I begged.

"Oh, like I'm going to tell you." She poked my shoulder.
"My mom wants to talk to your mom."

"Why?"

"She just does."

We went inside, and I leaned on the railing of the staircase while Amanda put her present in the den. "Mom!" I
yelled. "Mrs. Wilson needs you!"

"Winnie, please," Mom said. "I'm right here." She clopped
down the stairs in her low-heel shoes. "Hello, Amanda. I
like that shirt you're wearing."

I looked at Amanda's shirt—white with purple stripes—
and for a second I wished I'd worn something other than my
McDonald's shirt with a picture of a Big Mac on the front.
Oh, well. Another car pulled into the drive, and Amanda and
I dashed back out.

"It's Chantelle," Amanda said. She waved. "Chantelle, hi!"

Chantelle is Amanda's and my second-best friend. We
met her on the first day of third grade, when Mrs. Katcher
tried to guess what everyone's name was. Mrs. Katcher kept
frowning at Chantelle and trying new names, until finally
she put down her roll book and said, "Sweetheart, I give up!
There aren't any more boy's names left!"

Amanda and I found Chantelle during morning recess

and told her Mrs. Katcher was crazy. Didn't she know girls cut their hair short, too? We told Chantelle she looked sophisticated, like a model, and Chantelle smiled and lifted her head from her arms.

Now Chantelle's hair reaches almost to her shoulders, and today she held it back with a big, silver barrette that matched her silver earrings. She handed me a small box wrapped in shiny red paper and said, "Here. Happy birthday."

"Thanks," I said. "I'll put it inside with Amanda's."

Chantelle bumped Amanda's hip. "Is it . . . you know?"

"Is it *what?*" I demanded.

"Yes, but shhh," Amanda said. To me, she added, "And don't try to worm it out of her."

"Hi, everyone!" called Dinah Devine as she struggled out of her dad's station wagon. She wore a bright pink party dress, and her hair was pushed back with a matching plastic headband. Her smile stretched too wide across her face.

"Here," she said. "Happy birthday." She held out her present, a lumpy package tied with yarn.

"Thanks," I said. Dinah is somebody I try to be nice to at school, but I wouldn't have invited her to my party except Mom said I had to. Her dad works with my dad, which in Mom's mind meant Dinah should be included.

But along with her too-wide smile, Dinah is one of those people who laughed too late when someone makes a joke, or too loud, or too long, like, "Ha, ha! That was so hysterical!" even when the joke was really dumb. And if someone says something mean, like "We weren't talking to *you*," or "You don't even get it, do you?" Dinah never says anything back. Although one time she told our teacher, which was a mistake. Then the kids called her a tattletale, too.

Dinah's mom died when Dinah was a baby, which was really sad. I try to remember that. But sometimes the whole mess of it wears me out.

A car horn honked, and Dinah jumped. We moved to the edge of the driveway, and Louise's mom pulled up with Louise and Karen in the backseat. Louise and Karen are best friends, the kind who wear matching outfits to school and loop identical friendship bracelets around their wrists. Today Louise had on blue overalls and a white shirt, while Karen was wearing white overalls with a blue shirt. Karen trailed Louise up the driveway and smiled as Louise said hello for both of them.

"What now?" Louise said after we went inside and deposited their presents with others.

"Well," I announced, "we have very exciting plans. *Shockingly* exciting. Right, Amanda?"

"Shockingly," agreed Amanda.

I glanced from face to face. "I am pleased to inform you that tonight we will be performing a play written by yours truly. It is a dreadful and chilling play. It's called *The True Tale of Sophia-Maria: A Tragedy*."

Eleven

Louise frowned.

Dinah looked concerned.

"Who's Sophia-Maria?" Karen asked.

"Sophia-Maria is a girl exactly our age," I said. "She has lustrous black curls and violet eyes, and she never did anyone a moment's harm. But sadly, she is snatched from her home and taken to France, where she becomes a scullery maid for a horrible baroness."

"A scullery maid?" Karen repeated.

Louise sighed in a very loud way. "No offense, but could we *please* not put on one of your plays? You always get to be the heroine, and the rest of us get stuck being butlers or ladies-in-waiting."

"I get to be the heroine because I made it up," I explained. "But you can be the horrible baroness if you want. She's hunchbacked from riding camels, and she lisps."

"I don't want to be the baroness," she said. "I don't want to be anything."

This was a problem with Louise. She could be extremely difficult. I tried to appear agreeable while at the same time indicating with my tone that Louise was being a spoilsport. "Well, what *do* you want to do?"

"We could give each other makeovers," Chantelle said.

"Karen's mom won't let her wear makeup," Louise said. "Not until she's in junior high."

"Maybe that telephone game?" Dinah said. "Where

everybody whispers something into the next person's ear and it comes out all silly?"

"Wait," I said, sensing my plans slip from my grasp. "In the play there's a plague, did I tell you? Sophia-Maria gets horrible boils, and—"

"I know!" Louise said. "Do you still have that electric chair? The one that old lady used to use?"

"What old lady?" Karen asked.

"Mrs. Robinson," I said. "The lady who lived here before us. But—"

Karen's eyes grew big. "She had an electric chair?"

"Not *that* kind," Louise said. "Not where you get electrocuted. Tell them, Winnie."

I told them how Mrs. Robinson couldn't move around very well because she was, like, ninety years old, so she had an electric chair installed in the back staircase. It's an ugly vinyl chair connected to a steel track, and under the arm of the chair is a button, kind of like a doorbell. When you press it, the chair travels up the track. Or down the track, if you start at the top.

"It's not that exciting," I finished.

"It's better than doing a play," Louise said. She headed for the kitchen, and the others followed. By the time I caught up with them, they were crowded around the foot of the back staircase with Louise perched on the cracked vinyl seat.

"Everyone watching?" Louise asked. She punched the

"start" button, and the chair lurched up the stairs, motor whining. We heard a thunk when the chair got to the top, and Karen shrieked.

"It's okay," Louise called. "It always does that." The motor whirred and down came Louise, sitting proudly like a queen.

"Now you," she said to Karen.

Karen hesitated, then climbed onto the chair. "Like this?" she said. She pressed the button and squealed as the chair started back up the stairs.

"Mrs. Robinson?" I said, raising my voice to be heard over the motor. "The lady who lived here? She was so old she *died* in this house. My sister Sandra was afraid to move in because of ghosts."

That wasn't exactly true. Sandra was just trying to scare me.

"I *think* she died in the electric chair," I said even louder.

"Ooo!" everyone cried.

"Karen, you're sitting on a ghost!"

"Karen and ghostie, sitting in a tree!"

"Hey, I want to sit on the ghost!"

"Me, too!"

"Hurry up, Karen! You're squishing the ghostie!"

Karen climbed down, and Chantelle and Amanda got on to do a partner ride, with Amanda sitting in the seat of the chair and Chantelle balanced on one of the arms. Then

Karen went again, although she still didn't have the hang of it. She kept letting go of the "start" button, making the chair stall out. She giggled each time, and the others yelled, "Karen! Push the *button!*"

Louise reclaimed the chair, and I sat down on the lowest step, wrestling with my disappointment. It wasn't that I wanted to be the boss of everyone, but I'd worked hard on *The True Tale of Sophia-Maria*. I'd seen in my mind how it would be performed, and how afterward, as everybody congratulated me, I would blush modestly and say, "It was nothing. I just like to make stuff up."

And it *was* a heart-wrenching story. Sophia-Maria lost three fingers due to the plague, and the baroness cast her into the street with nothing but a tattered gray shawl. She had no friends, and she wandered the earth singing mournful songs. Finally she was killed by a pack of wild javelinas, and when everyone found out, they felt terrible for not treating her more nicely. The last line of the play, to be delivered by the butler, was, "For the welfare of all children, for the consideration of poor, innocent girls and boys, and for the bettering of your community as a whole, I beg you: BE KIND TO A STRANGER TODAY!"

Louise clunked to a halt at the bottom of the staircase. "*That's* how you do it," she said to Karen.

"Can I have a turn?" Dinah asked.

"No," said Louise.

"Why not?"

"Because."

I roused myself from my slump. Dinah's eyes had a rab-bity look to them, and her cheeks were pink.

"Yes, you can have a turn," I told Dinah. "Louise, get off."

"I'm not done yet," Louise said.

"You've gone twice already. You've got to share."

Louise hesitated, then hopped down as if she'd never cared in the first place. "You better not break it," she said to Dinah.

Dinah climbed onto the seat and squeezed her knees together. She pressed the button and off she went.

"Okay," I said when she was done. I slapped my hands on my thighs and stood up. "Everyone's had a turn. Let's go to the kitchen and—"

"Hey!" Louise protested. "Karen and I haven't gone double!"

Chantelle pushed her way forward. "I bet if someone helped me I could do a handstand on the—"

"*My* turn to go next—"

"—not fair, because you already—"

"But don't you guys want to eat?" I asked. "We're going to have pizza, and everyone gets to put on their own toppings."

No one paid attention.

"Amanda?" I pleaded. "Aren't you hungry?"

Amanda stopped arguing, and I could tell she'd finally remembered our plans. She stepped toward me. "I love pizza," she said.

"Me, too," said Chantelle.

Louise put her hands on her hips. "Yeah, but—"

"Come on," I said before she could finish. "Last one to the kitchen is a rotten egg."

Originally Mom wanted to stay in the kitchen to supervise, but I told her no, I could take care of dinner myself.

"Here's how it works," I told everyone. "We've got two crusts. Me and Amanda and Chantelle will make this one, and Louise and Karen and Dinah, you can make the other. The toppings are on the counter, and the sauce is in the blue bowl by the sink."

I pulled Amanda and Chantelle toward the counter. My chest felt lighter now that we were back on track. "What should we do?" I asked. "Green pepper and onion? Or, I know! We could make a smiley face, with pepperoni for eyes and a green pepper for the mouth!"

"Not too much green pepper," Chantelle said. "I don't mind a little, but not, like, all over the whole thing."

"That's why I said for the mouth. There's only one mouth."

A worry line formed on Amanda's forehead, and I stopped talking and followed her gaze. At the end of the counter Louise and Karen were sprinkling cheese onto their pizza while Dinah stood to the side, biting her thumbnail.

"Dinah, why aren't you helping?" I asked.

Dinah pulled her thumb out of her mouth and wiped it on her dress. "Um . . ."

"She doesn't like pepperoni," Louise said. She grabbed a handful of pepperoni slices and scattered them over the cheese.

"So split the pizza in thirds," I said.

Louise mushed the pepperonis into the sauce. "Too late."

Dinah gave a wobbly smile. "I can eat pepperoni. I don't mind."

My heart started beating too fast. "You guys," I said to Louise and Karen. "You can't hog that whole pizza to yourselves."

"Who says we're hogging?"

The silence stretched out. I was afraid I was going to cry, or that it would *look* like I was going to cry, which would be just as bad. Why did Louise have to act so snotty? And why couldn't Dinah handle it on her own?

"Fine," I said. "Come on, Dinah, I'll switch with you."

"Wait," Amanda said. She touched my arm. "I'll go."

Amanda joined Karen and Louise, and Dinah stepped up behind me and Chantelle. "I don't mind pepperoni," she said in a voice that was barely there. "We can put it on if you want."

I didn't answer. I plucked off the pepperoni eyeballs and dropped them into the sink.

"But—" Chantelle said.

"We'll use mushrooms instead," I said. I didn't meet her gaze.

ⓖ ⓖ ⓖ

After pizza we had cake, because Mom forgot we were supposed to open presents first, and once she brought the cake out, it was too late to take it back. When everyone was done eating, we moved into the den and settled down on the sofa and the floor.

"That's quite a stash you've got there," Dad said, nodding at the gifts piled up on the coffee table. "Sure they're all for you?"

"D-a-ad," I said. I pressed my palms on my legs and tried to get that birthday feeling back. I reached for the box from Amanda, but she shook her head.

"Mine last," she said.

I picked up the package beside it and read the card: "'Happy Birthday, Winnie. Love, Louise.' And, oh, there's a puppy dog holding a balloon." I held out the card for the others to see, and everyone made oohing sounds like they wished that puppy were right here with us.

I tore the paper from the box. "Body glitter!"

"You are *so* lucky," Amanda said.

"Pass it around," said Louise. I handed it to her, and she uncapped the tube.

Chantelle leaned forward. "Now open mine."

I peeled the paper from her present. "Earrings! They're beautiful!"

"They're clip-ons," Chantelle said, "but you can still wear them once you get your ears pierced."

I took the earrings off the card and put them on. They made my ears feel heavy when I moved my head.

"They make you look mature," Louise said. "Like thirteen at least."

"Clip-ons stretch out your ears," Karen warned.

"Not these," Chantelle said.

"They look very nice," Mom said. She won't let me pierce my ears until I'm twelve, but these she couldn't complain about because they were a gift.

"Here, open this one," Amanda said, pushing Karen's present at me. From inside the box I pulled out a set of Bonne Bell Lip-Smackers in all different flavors. The set included five normal Lip-Smackers, plus one huge one with a cord through the top so I could wear it around my neck. Its flavor was "Dr Pepper," and it smelled exactly like Dr Pepper.

From Dinah I got a scrunchy with gold stars on it. "I made it myself," she said, scrunching the hem of her dress. "I can do it over if you don't like the color."

"No, gold's okay," I said. "Thanks."

Finally, Amanda handed me her present.

"It feels empty," I said.

"Open it," Amanda said.

"Open it!" the others cried.

I ripped off the wrapping paper and lifted the lid from the box. Inside lay a card. "'Happy Birthday, Winnie,'" I read aloud. "'Will you take care of me?'" I peered into the box again. There was nothing there. "I don't get it. Take care of what?"

From the doorway came a squeaky meow. Mom was holding a tiny gray-and-white kitten, its whole body smaller than one of my dad's sneakers. The kitten meowed again, and everyone said, "Ohh!"

I jumped up and ran to Mom. "To keep? Really?"

Mom nodded. "Amanda's mother brought her by when she dropped off Amanda."

I turned to Amanda. "Oh, thank you! Thank you, thank you, thank you!" I took the kitten from Mom's arms.

"She's a girl," Amanda said. "Isn't she adorable?"

"Hi," I said to the kitten. "This is where you live now, okay?" She climbed up my chest and pushed at my neck with her head.

"Happy birthday, squirt," Dad said. He came forward and tousled my hair. "We'll leave you girls alone to enjoy your presents. Holler if you need anything."

He and Mom left the room, and I sat down on the floor with my kitten.

"What are you going to name her?" asked Chantelle.

"How about Socks?" Karen said.

"Or Mittens," said Louise, "because of her teensy white feet. And because it rhymes with kitten."

Chantelle wrinkled her nose. "Mittens the kitten?"

I thought for a moment, then said, "Sweetie-Pie."

"Like Sweet-Pea, Amanda's cat!" said Chantelle.

"Yep. They're sisters."

"Adopted sisters," Amanda said. She grinned.

We watched as Sweetie-Pie licked her back leg. Her tongue made spiky spots on her fur.

"Well?" Louise asked. "Is that all?"

"All what?" I said.

"All the presents."

"Yeah, I guess, but—"

"So what are we waiting for?" She stood up and tightened her ponytail. "Let's go play on the electric chair!"

"Yeah!" said Karen.

"Me first!" cried Chantelle as she dashed for the door.

"Nuh-uh!" Louise said. "It was my idea!"

Their feet pounded the floor as they ran down the hall, everyone but me. I heard the whine of the chair's motor, followed by a burst of laughter. Someone must have tried a new trick. Or maybe whoever it was fell off. I hoped it was Louise.

I held Sweetie-Pie close and rubbed my cheek against hers. "You don't want to ride on that stupid chair, do you?" I whispered. "Huh?"

Sweetie-Pie squirmed free. She padded across the room, sniffing in the direction of the back hall.

"She's so cute," Dinah said, appearing at the door. She knelt and scooped Sweetie-Pie into her arms.

"Why aren't you riding the chair?" I asked. It came out sounding mean, and my face grew hot.

"It's boring," she said. "Plus, Louise won't let me. She says I'm too big."

"Louise is a turd. Anyway, my dad's ridden on it and he's way bigger than you."

She sat down beside me. "It's just a chair."

Sweetie-Pie settled into Dinah's lap. From her chest came a tiny purr.

"She likes you," I said grudgingly.

"I have four cats at home," Dinah said. "Gypsy, Muffet, Buffy, and Katzy. They like to be scratched behind their ears, like this." She demonstrated. "Go ahead. Try."

I scratched behind Sweetie-Pie's ears, and her purrs grew louder. From the hall came another burst of giggles, and Dinah and I glanced at each other. She looked anxious, like she thought I might leave.

"We could try out my new Lip-Smackers," I suggested, shifting my gaze.

"You mean it?" Dinah asked. "They're brand-new."

"They're going to have to get used sometime." I grabbed the Lip-Smackers from the table and lined them up, the fruit-flavored ones first and then the giant Dr Pepper at the end. I chose a white one called Coconut Crazy and smoothed it over my lips.

Dinah pointed to a red one called Strawberry Dream. "Can I try this one?"

"Smell it first to make sure you like it."

She held it up to her nose. "I think I like it. Do you?"

I took a quick sniff. "Yeah. It smells good."

She raised it to her lips, crossing her eyes to keep it in sight.

Today I am eleven, I said to myself. *Eleven years old.* From down the hall I heard Karen yell that she was being squished, followed by Louise calling her a baby. In Dinah's lap, Sweetie-Pie continued to purr. I uncapped another Lip-Smacker—Bursting with Blueberries—and breathed in deep.